THE FIRST CRACK

by JSD Johnston

THE FIRST CRACK
Tomo 1, parsa iii
of Peyton Drake's Omni Tale
by JSD Johnston

IMMERSIVE EDITION
interactive elements available only from OmniTales.net

Welcome back to Peyton Drake's Omni Tale, a coming-of-age saga told in 49 novella installments, compiled into 7 full-length series. Pete's tale is serialized and meant to be read sequentially. So if you've not yet read novellas one (*Marked for Adventure*) and two (*Destiny by Design*), toddle off and return once you're up to speed.

Omni Tales are meant to serve as catalysts for assorted interactive experiences, both online and in person. This novella comes with tactile inserts, and the PDF contains links to dozens of digital content pieces including secret info, author narrations, Omnopoly chapter games with digital rewards, coloring pages, our Bells & Whistles book club packet with trivia, and more. If you're reading this but don't have access to all of the above, write to us at genie@omniocademy.com and we'll get you sorted.

Copyright © 2016/2023 by JSD Johnston
All rights reserved.
ISBN: 978-1-959822-02-8
Library of Congress Control Number: 2023915980
Published in Long Beach, CA

Published by E. Gads Hill Press
KRAKEN INK

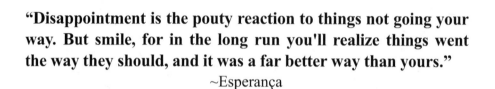

"Disappointment is the pouty reaction to things not going your way. But smile, for in the long run you'll realize things went the way they should, and it was a far better way than yours."

~Esperança

THE MATTER

continued from Tomo 1, parsa ii – Destiny by Design

"You can put your arms down now," the fellow said, removing Pete's blindfold. "Welcome home, mate."

Pete blinked in disbelief, and his vision narrowed to a small circle as he watched a group of more than a hundred students jump up and down, cheering and chanting his name.

His pancreas threatened to escape through his nose.

He may not have found his element, but for better or worse, his element had most certainly found him.

THE END

of Pete's Appraisement

{Kapta Fuinenn-An}

CHAPTER THIRTY-ONE – THE LIQUID THICKENS

Pete Drake's heart had dropped into his stomach and rattled around there for a spell when he realized he was back in the Crux, the arena at the Academy of Omniosophical Arts & Sciences that he'd visited twice in the last two days, both times with nightmarish results. After surviving the grueling multiday assessment known as the Appraisement Cycle, he'd arrived at the pivotal moment when he would find out which of the interdimensional school's element domains was to provide his new home, social circle, and sense of identity.

The better part of the student crowd sat clapping politely when Pete's name was announced. One group was on its feet, pogoing and crowing in jubilation. Pete marked their matching teal raglan shirts, but had a hard time making out the element emblem on the front of the shirts while everyone jumped around.

His worst fears were realized when he espied Edni (the oceanid recruit on whom he had a crush) among those cheering. Gripped with dread, he looked down at his torso and confirmed he'd been outfitted in the same teal raglan shirt while he was blindfolded—a shirt silkscreened with a large symbol of an ocean wave.

The unthinkable had happened. He had been bonded to Aquis, the water domain that had lurked at the bottom of his list of element preferences. Even his joy at seeing Edni and being in the same domain as she couldn't allay his misery.

"Tena koe, bugalugs," said the voice of the person who had led Pete up onto the Crux stage, slid the shirt over Pete's arms, and removed Pete's blindfold. "Sorry for the quaking hands. I'm a tad nervous – as if you couldn't tell. Bonzers meeting ya, Drake! I'm Kyrian, your podmate."

Pete turned around to look up into the face of the most perfect human specimen he'd ever seen. Kyrian was statuesque and athletically built, with classically handsome features, kind aqua eyes, collar-length dark wavy hair, and a beguiling smile. Pete gulped. "I'm Pete."

"I reckon someone's gotta be," his new roommate quipped with a grin. "Alley-oop. Let's get you into your element."

Kyrian ushered him to a pair of seats in the Aquis section of the Crux where Pete was showered with pats on the back, hugs, and boisterous applause. Edni waved from several rows back and clasped her hands in a victory gesture. Pete waved back, forcing a smile.

In Pete's mind, his element assignment was outside the realm of possibility. More to the point, it was lunacy. He enjoyed the Wonders Under the Sea dance hosted by Aquis during Appraisement, but that was mainly because of Edni. Other than that, his impressions of the water domain were far from positive.

As each recruit was unblindfolded and wrapped in the bosom of his new element family, Pete clapped mindlessly, cheering more feverishly when a recruit joined the Aquis ranks, just to appear a team player. He hatched plans to get reassigned, or even kicked out of the academy and sent home if things became desperate. Someone somewhere had made a mistake. That's all there was to it.

When the final recruit was welcomed, general pandemonium broke out, with every element section trying to be louder than the next. The students in each domain sang their canticle (traditional song), or more aptly, screamed it from the top of their lungs, swaying side to side, whistling, gesturing proudly, and carrying on like out-of-control seven-year-olds who'd consumed excessive amounts of sugar.

The ringmaster helming the proceedings hopped onto the stage wearing a Nitris logo shirt in place of the circus getup he'd worn earlier, still carrying his ringmaster's whip. After much effort, he quieted the mob. "Hule huli to all you neophytes for getting through the most punishing auction since the Unexpected Inquisition. We're looking forward to great things from you new Fids. Make your elements proud." Several recruits wiped tears from their eyes—Pete couldn't tell if the tears signified happiness or heartbreak. "I formally declare the auction of sekkl dyiH-be closed!" The ringmaster twirled the long whip over his head and gave it a sharp crack. The crowd cheered once more.

Kyrian placed the blindfold back over Pete's eyes. "Just until we get there."

Pete was too flabbergasted to object. He and the other blindfolded Aquis newcomers were ushered out of the Crux, down a dank hallway, and onto a dock where they were helped into some sort of tippy vessels which he guessed were canoes. Pete considered faking a sprained ankle in hopes of being sent to Healers Bay where he could strategize a plan to be reassigned to another element.

Unfortunately, Kyrian was coordinated enough for both of them and effortlessly got Pete seated and squared away, despite the blindfold and waffling watercraft. In silence, the skiffs glided through a small underground waterway until they arrived in the lake of a large grotto.

"You may take your blindfolds off now," a gentle female voice said.

Pete opened his mouth to make some sort of excuse as to why he needed to go back to his recruit room, but when he slid the fabric off his eyes, he was rendered dumbstruck and unable to utter a syllable.

Floating oil lamps surrounded the canoes, dotting the inky liquid canvas with light, bobbing as each craft cut through the water. Beneath the surface, luminescent fish lit up the depths, swimming in choreographed formation, at turns leaping into the air and splashing those in the boats. Even the grotto's walls glimmered, with speckles of radiance generated by the glowworms that lived in the rock.

A barge set with eight long tables rested in the midst of the lake under a canopy of aerated moon jellies that drifted high overhead, their lengthy tentacles embellished with glitter for the occasion. In the middle of the barge stood a vertical ice sculpture in the shape of a man-sized fish with eyes that blinked and cheeks that puffed when it periodically spouted a stream of turquoise water. Each table was overlain with fishnets and decorated with flickering seashell candles along with hefty centerpieces of variegated corals from the Borderless Reef.

Of all the stunning sights Pete had witnessed since coming to the academy, this scene affected him the most. Its simple and sublime beauty gripped his throat and brought tears to his eyes. He'd always teased his mother about how she would turn maudlin when viewing a fiery sunset or listening to Beethoven's *Ode to Joy*. He wouldn't be teasing her anymore.

"Punch?" asked a boy who resembled Mr. Limpet, an anthropomorphic fish character from an animated film Pete liked as a tyke.

Pete nodded eagerly, accepting a crystal bubble filled with Barely Berry Whizbang Punch, a beverage he'd first tried at the flying carpet picnic he'd attended in Nitris (the air domain) during Appraisement. The drink had become an instant favorite of his, and he'd been unable to procure any since the picnic.

Finally!

He grabbed his bubble with both hands, swallowing the fizzy drink in great gulps.

Kyrian placed a tempering hand on Pete's forearm. "It's for sipping during the welcome speeches. You don't want to chug it, trust me. It'll send you rocketing off the grotto walls."

Pete nodded and put the bubble down, remembering the gaseous effects the punch had on diners at the Nitris picnic.

The first person to stand and speak was one of the estate Caretakers, Fenella Jetty. Hers was an emotive speech, laden with remorse over the absence of the Aquins who remained trapped in Oblivion, victims of the Dimension Kappa Kidnapping perpetrated by the rebel group known as XQ, short for Exaequos. When her welcome remarks came to a close, everyone crossed their wrists and rapidly snapped their fingers one hand at a time in appreciation, thereafter taking a temperate sip of punch.

Fenella then introduced Skylar Krestan, one of Aquis' two Squallix Shapers. Aquins old and new cheered. Pete assumed the term *Shaper* meant Skylar was a coach for the water sport called Squallix, an activity Pete knew nothing about, aside from its name as listed in the Piddlypedia student handbook.

Fenella shared how Skylar had played Squallix quasi-professionally and had been on track to bump up to the Archipelagian League before his career was cut short by an injury resulting from an altercation with a hippopotamus that believed Skylar was flirting with its mate. The word *hippopotamus* was one of the few Pete understood.

"Felilum, fingerlings and friends," a trilling high-pitched voice said.

Pete looked around for the speaker, but saw only husky, hirsute Skylar standing. By the time Pete realized the girlish voice was coming from Skylar, the crowd was again snapping and sipping, and Skylar took his seat.

The final toast came from Demetrius, the hulking student whom Pete first encountered during the tsunami incident when Pete and his co-recruits rode dolphins on the Aquis sea during the Appraisement estate tours. Demetrius was a Scion (designated student leader) and looked to be about twenty years of age. Aside from his brawn and overall physical impressiveness, Demetrius possessed a natural charisma and had an aura of innate goodness. With impassioned sincerity he disclosed how vigorously Aquis had fought to induct each of the new recruits into their ranks. "And that means you," he said, looking Pete square in the eye, or so Pete thought or, at least, hoped.

Pete snapped with extra zeal.

Once Demetrius resumed his seat, mollifying music rose up from the water where a pygmy beluga quartet sang in four-part harmony. As the whales crooned, eight mermaids swam toward the barge, their opalescent hands carrying abalone shells above their heads. Each shell was filled with shrimp gazpacho, served as the first course of what was to be a sumptuous feast.

After the soup, jumbo clamshells brimming with kelp salad floated out to the barge. Pete was about as keen on kelp as he'd been on kale at home, and merely moved it around his plate with his trident-style fork without really eating any, hoping no one would observe his subterfuge.

A bale of turtles swam out next, their backs laden with mother-of-pearl platters heaped with lobster ravioli. Fruit salad followed, served in sailboats constructed of halved pineapples with banana leaf sails. In between courses, the diners tossed their dirty dinnerware into the lake where a battalion of candy-striped Plecostomus waited to feed on the remnants and pick clean the plates.

One thing I'll say for these Aquis people, I like the way they do dishes!

Just when Pete was sure he could eat no more, a dozen bonnet rays approached the barge bearing on their wings coconut shells filled with coconut-Macadamia ice cream garnished with Madeleines partially dipped in dark chocolate. Pete was in epicurean Nirvana and devoured every morsel proffered.

Dad always complains I'm too skinny – looks like that won't be a problem anymore.

Throughout the festivities, Kyrian kept a close eye on his charge, making a point to serve Pete before serving himself, introducing him to more people than Pete could remember. Pete had never had someone take him under their wing before. It felt wonderful.

Why couldn't Kyrian have been from Platen instead, Pete thought, having hoped to be bonded to Platen, the metal element.

When the meal concluded, a baby blue whale silently rose to the surface next to the barge, eliciting gasps of deference from the recruits who were instructed to walk across the aquatic mammal's back over to a shoal illuminated by starfish holding tiny lanterns. There, the newcomers were given sheets of dried seaweed on which were written the Aquis credo. Each plebe was expected to memorize the words while waiting in line to have his forehead permanently stamped with the Aquis emblem—a stamp that would only be visible when viewed with an Ultra-Aetherean light source.

Instead of learning the credo, Pete spent his time in line trying to think of a way to get out of Aquis.

Maybe I could say I'm allergic to water?

He was determined not to like his assigned element or its people, but so far, every Aquin he'd met had been warm and friendly—none more so than his imminent roommate Kyrian who at first blush appeared to be everything Pete could ask for in a friend. And of course, Edni was in Aquis.

At the moment, his chief concern was the prospect of having his forehead permanently stamped.

Permanent sounds so permanent!

He whittled his thumbnails, bedeviled by visions of a white-hot branding iron searing his face. Any minute he expected the lull of the lapping waves to be pierced by a shriek of agony from a recruit being stamped. After advancing several places in line without hearing a single blood-curdling reaction, he concluded the stamping process was painless—either that or all those who went before him had sky-high pain thresholds—or had passed out.

As the recruits prepared for their rite of passage, the older students packed up the Plecos-scrubbed banquet dishes and took down the tables, leaving the barge empty of everything but sanguine Aquins. When all of the newbies had been stamped, they huddled together on the sandbar, anxiously awaiting whatever might befall them next.

"Who wants to go first?" Caretaker Fenella called out, her previously somber mood having turned to giggly silliness. Pete chalked up her change in attitude to an excess of Barely Berry Whizbang Punch.

Without a moment's hesitation, Kyrian dove into the water toward the sandbar. A couple of strokes later, he emerged, his soaked tee shirt and trousers clinging to his muscular frame.

"Oh my!" Fenella said, fanning herself as she regarded Kyrian.

Kyrian waded toward Pete, smiling. "Off with the shoes."

Pete's apprehension made moving his feet difficult. Kyrian knelt down and removed Pete's shoes for him, flinging them back over his shoulder in the direction of the barge where Demetrius easily caught them. Kyrian then stood and held out his hand to Pete. Pete took it automatically, clumsily following Kyrian who backed into the water until Pete was in up to his waist.

Kyrian looked into Pete's eyes and quietly asked, "You positive you wanna spend the next seven seekkl of your life with this mangy waterlogged lot? Think charily before answering. If you say aye, there's no changing your answer later if you tire of us by end of term. If you say nay, well, your Aquis stamp won't fully cure for another four duraa and you can still have it removed and entreat another domain … or even return home if you want …"

Unintentionally, Pete audibly exhaled in relief. He followed enough of the lingo to understand he could still get out of Aquis. He could still get out of all of it. All he had to do was say so.

"So what's it gonna be, Peyton Drake from Dimension Q?" Kyrian said with a warm smile.

Pete averted his eyes, chewing the inside of his bottom lip as he mulled over how best to request a transfer without being rude. His gaze fell on Edni who stood on the sandbar, her dainty hands clasped in front of her, the light from the floating candles making her amber eyes sparkle. She smiled at him with a look of sheer contentment.

Upon seeing that smile, Pete's die was cast.

He turned back and looking up into Kyrian's kindly face, simply nodded *yes*.

Kyrian grinned and nodded in turn, then spoke up for all to hear. "Peyton Drake, do you pledge to defend the values of the Academy of Omniosophical Arts and Sciences? Will you bind yourself, body and soul, to Omni and to the elementum aquae with your brothers and sisters who have sworn the same?"

The grinning throng hung on Pete's response. He scanned the sea of robust sun-kissed surfers, mermaids, selkies, and naiads on the barge, all of whom he considered to be out of his league. He couldn't fathom why they would want someone as unexceptional as him to be part of their element family. But apparently, they did.

Again he nodded.

"Now say the words … loud."

Pete started to speak, but nothing came out. He tried again, and his voice boomed, much to the gratification of the veteran students who cheered their approval from the barge. Working his recent memory, Pete recited the credo. "Through tears of joy I entered the Omniverse. Through tears of mourning I shall depart it. Until that breathless moment, I commit my allegiance, my friendship, my industry, and my honor to serving and guarding the academy, the liquid realm, and all that abide therein."

"Good on ya, Fiddle Drake, well done!" Kyrian smiled and placed his hand on top of Pete's head before plunging him straight down into the water.

A moment later Pete shot up, gasping for air as the barge crowd snapped.

Kyrian mussed Pete's wet hair and said, "Cheriste som," the phrase (from the ancient language Naturim) that was used for a variety of reasons, rather like *aloha* in Hawaiian.

"Alo cheriste pless," Pete garbled, offering the expected Naturim response.

Kyrian cocked his head toward the barge. "Let's paddle."

It took Kyrian only a few effortless strokes to swim to the scow. Pete labored to get there without holding his nose or making a huge flailing fool of himself. When he got to the float's edge, Kyrian was already up on the barge. He lifted Pete with one hand and wrapped him in a large towel emblazoned with the Aquis logo.

Pete felt instantly relaxed and relieved to be done with the ordeal, especially because his forehead felt no discomfort from having been stamped. He watched with interest as each recruit transformed into a bona fide Aquin. Without exception, all were treated with equal warmth and respect—even those who might normally be classified as runts or outcasts.

Kids here are treated so much better than at school back home.

He snuggled deeper into his plush towel, more at ease than he'd felt in years.

I think maybe I did the right thing after all.

With the induction of the last recruit, the mob engaged in unbridled cavorting that threatened to capsize the barge.

"What now?" Pete asked Kyrian as a pair of stocky water trolls pulled the wherry to shore.

"Orientation," Kyrian answered with a wicked grin.

"I thought the student handbook said academy orientation was tomorrow."

"Not Ocademy orientation." Kyrian drummed his fingers together, his expression turning more impish. "*Aquis* orientation."

Pete's pancreas kicked his spleen. He never knew the word *orientation* could conjure such trepidation.

{Kapta Fuinenn-Be}

CHAPTER THIRTY-TWO – OF PODS & PINS

The 166 inhabitants of the Aquis estate trudged through a series of damp tiki-torch-lit caves. The energy drain of Pete's harrowing Appraisement Cycle saga now caught up to him, and he felt certain he would fall asleep while walking. Drifting in and out of semi-consciousness, he once again recalled that he had yet to contact his parents since stealing away from home in the middle of the night to come to the academy. The only consolation was the fact there would be no doubt as to his whereabouts. Most likely his mother had long since confessed her involvement in his escape anyway, having provided the parental signature required for Pete to travel through the school's portal.

When the congregation emerged from the caves, Pete was surprised to find they were back in Aquis' omnipurpose room where the Wonders Under the Sea dance had been held just a few days prior. He endeavored to scan the crowd for Edni, but being as he lived on the short end of the height spectrum, he saw little more than chests and midriffs and Aquis logos.

Once everyone had filed into the hall, the new Fiddleheads (*Fiddleheads* being the academy term for students) were instructed to sit on the floor facing a seven-inch-high twelve-foot-square freshwater aquarium topped by a stage. The new Fiddleheads' older podmates sat behind them.

Aquis orientation consisted of a series of elaborate skits performed by both students and Stipes (onsite staff). The first presentation gave an overview of the proud and illustrious history of the element. Tired as Pete was, he remained rapt throughout, awed by the tales of water gods and the descriptions of water's power to shape worlds and sustain life.

The historical sketch was followed by a morality play about the tragedies of speciesism. Students were advised that prejudice whether on the part of humans, merfolk, naiads, selkies, undine, kelpies, sea monsters, et cetera would not be tolerated. The leaders of feuding salt water and fresh water clans were brought up on stage to make peace. They each poured a glass of water—one salt, one fresh—into a shared basin, then washed their face and hands in the hybrid solution as a symbolic gesture. Thereafter, they exchanged lotus leis and hugs. The audience gave them a snapping ovation.

The last skit dealt with far lighter subject matter, offering the newcomers a comic look at daily life at the boarding school. The Stipes then introduced themselves, saving for last the heroes of the domains, the Galleymasters who were greeted with affectionate snapping. Finally, Caretaker Fenella announced the term's Scion appointments, asking the new Scions and their assistants to stand. Thereafter, she dismissed the assemblage to find their rooms.

To Pete's relief, the presentation proved to be far more innocuous than he anticipated.

Kyrian stood and stretched. "What'd ya think?"

"That was way less – I dunno – scary than I was expecting."

"Yeah, we like to put the fear of Deora into the new Fids before orientation. Helps keep 'em awake during the slow bits. Alley-oop," Kyrian extended a hand to Pete then guided him down a corridor that led to a corkscrew staircase beside which spiraled a water slide.

Pete's weary legs took exception to the idea of the staircase and refused to participate in its ascension. "Umm, where's the elevator?"

"Pfft, sounds like you paid a visit to Arbis or Nitris," Kyrian said, climbing the steep steps backward. "Pansy buggers think they're too lofty for stairs. That's why they have no lower body strength –

don't think they need it for flying and swinging through trees. This winding old staircase and I have been through a lot together. I run the steps to help me train."

Pete was tempted to ask what exactly Kyrian trained for, but he suspected he didn't want to hear the answer as it almost certainly involved athletics—the sort of activity Pete vehemently shunned. Besides, all of Pete's energy was going into his thighs and calves at the moment—his mouth couldn't have formed a question if it tried.

When at last they reached the landing and entrance of their Frond (one of each element domain's two housing units), Pete stopped to view the layout—and to rest. The arrangement looked exactly as he'd pictured based on the diagram in the *Piddlypedia* student welcome circular he'd received his first day.

Wow, this is all really happening.

He and Kyrian had just passed the six Stipe rooms situated at the front of the Frond, when Kyrian darted left down a short hallway, stopping at the first door on the right. "This is us," he said, crooking his thumb toward the nameplate on the door.

Kyrian Parata (Dim Theta) – Warden

Peyton Drake (Dim Q) – Ward

"Ohhhhhh so that's what a Warden is," Pete said, having wondered about the meaning of the term since reading it in *Piddlypedia*. "*You* are my Warden."

"Yip, and you're my Ward." Kyrian smiled and opened the door for Pete.

Pete tiptoed into the room. "Whoaaaaa."

The accommodation was compact and sparse, but to the fourteen-year-old from planet Gaia (aka Earth) in Dimension Q, it was better than a palace. Two roll-top desks stood on either side of the chamber, above which hung a pair of hammocks.

"Is that where we sleep?"

"Sure is."

"Cooooool. But how do we get up there?"

Kyrian gestured toward a graduated series of box drawers attached to each desk. "They double as stairs."

Pete nodded in rapturous approval. The inventor in him appreciated the furniture's clever design.

At the far end of the chamber stood an armoire, similar to the one Pete had used in his temporary recruit quarters, though the new one was much larger and more elaborate with a cupboard comprising the center section and mirrored doors on either side.

"We each get a cubby," Kyrian said, opening one of the side doors. "The middle part belongs to our valet, and for your own sake, you do *not* want to touch his stuff."

Pete would've been shocked at the notion of having a valet had it not been for Sable, the silent little orb robot that attended to him during Appraisement.

The center door of the armoire opened quietly, and a shiny cobalt orb about one-and-a-half times the size of Sable floated out, somewhat wider than it was tall. The gleaming robot wore a striped waistcoat, an Aquis logo bow tie, a black derby hat, and white gloves.

"How do you do, syr?" it said to Pete, removing the derby and dusting it off.

"Whoa, you talk?" Pete said.

The android hung its hat on the armoire's center hook and adjusted the Aquis bow tie. "Yes, syr, I do indeed possess the gift of speech in a myriad of languages, binary being my programmed vernacular."

"Very cool."

"Would you like me to turn up the thermostat, syr?" the robot said in response to Pete's *cool* comment.

Kyrian chuckled.

"No, I mean … I'm Pete, by the way."

"Yes, Maistr Peyton, I have familiarized myself with your physiognomy and dossier. I am Ottomaton, however you may feel free to address me as Otto, if you find it simpler and preferable, syr."

"Very nice to make your acquaintance, Mr. Otto."

Kyrian put a foot on the lowest step of his box-stairs and bounded up into his hammock. Rolling onto his back, he pointed overhead to a fishing net attached at each corner to hooks on the ceiling. "We share that space. It's for Squallix equipment. Keeps it off the floor."

Pete felt the wind drop out of his sails. The only thing he knew about Squallix was that it was a sport. That was all he needed to know to be sure he wouldn't like it.

"Field player assigning is this plulum. I've been counting down the dura since last term. Looks like we're gonna have a pretty tough-to-beat roster this year."

"Great," Pete replied, feigning enthusiasm.

Hopefully "this plulum" means "later this decade."

"You play much Squallix in Dim Q?" Kyrian asked.

"Actually, I'd never heard of it until I got to the academy a few days ago," Pete said, his attention fixed on Otto who'd pulled out a large board from beneath the tabletop of Pete's desk and was setting clothing atop it. "I'd never even heard of the academy or the Omniverse or anything about other dimensions until a couple days before that."

"You're greener in the gills than I thought. How's it possible you didn't know anything about all *this* with Cassiopeia Salvatori as your mum?"

Pete was unaccustomed to hearing his mother referred to by her maiden name. He was unaccustomed to hearing his mother referred to at all! He regarded her as a meek and mild-mannered homemaker whose medication rendered her a bit slow and absentminded. But ever since first being approached to come to the interdimensional school, he'd heard references to her having been a hero admired by her peers during her own academy days.

He massaged the spot on his side where he believed his pancreas was located, sure it had just cramped.

I really need to learn about Mom's life when she was here.

"Drake?" Kyrian said, pulling Pete back into the conversation.

"Huh? Oh yeah, my mom, well I don't really know about the stuff academy people say about her. She had an accident before I was born and supposedly it changed her."

Kyrian propped himself up on one elbow. "Changed her? That's putting it gently. It's a ruddy miracle she's still alive. No one could've survived that attack."

Pete's pancreas cramped again. He considered asking about *that attack*, but feared the details would be more than he could bear at the moment.

"What's it like being the son of a savior?" Kyrian said.

Pete's pancreas did a flip. "Pardon?"

"Just having you on, since, you know, your mum's last name means savior."

No, I didn't know. In fact, I'm beginning to think I don't know much about Mom at all!

Pete labored to compose himself. "I'm used to her just being Mom," he said, then changed the subject. "Hey, I have a question. I noticed most of the dimensions have cool names like Theta or Omicron. How come my dimension is referred to as Q?"

"That's an easy one. It's cuz your dimension is so young. According to the legends, originally, there were no dimensions – only the Great All. When things splintered in modern times, modern meaning since Recorded Chronology, the first designated dimensions were named using letters from the Grecian alphabet. Greek was the lingua omniversal a while back. By the time your dimension came along, all of the Greco letters had been used up, and the newer dimensions were given letters from the modern People's Parlance."

"That's what we're speaking now, right?"

"Yip, what do *you* call it?"

"English."

Kyrian lay back and chuckled. "You Q-zers, what a funny breed you are."

Pete's mind instantly winged to the family's cross-country drive to their current Marine Corps base home. During their sojourn, they'd stopped at a diner where Pete encountered a girl whom he deemed suspicious and up to no good.

Q-zers, that's the word the girl at the diner said!

"Ahem," Otto interjected, producing a spherical chronometer from his waistcoat pocket. "Maistr Kyrian, would you care to give your Ward a tour of the Frond, syr?"

"I can tell this one's gonna be a pain in the gillbladder," Kyrian said with a wink, nodding toward Otto. "Alley-oop, Drake, let's take the grand tour. It should take all of thirty teekk."

Pete had learned during Appraisement that a *tekk* was a unit of time close to what he knew as a *second*. He was thrilled to think the tour of the dormitory would take only thirty *teekk*.

Kyrian leapt from his hammock as Otto opened the door to the shared bathroom.

"Looks like we're starting in the water closet." Kyrian gestured toward the open door. "Go on in."

Each of the washroom's four corners featured a commode enclosed by a hanging wave-patterned curtain. A sink flanked either side of the mirror-enclosed shower, and a double-length bathtub took up the empty space on the facing wall.

"That is by far the biggest bathtub I've ever seen," Pete said.

"For the merfolk, or should I say, for their tails." Kyrian said, leaning against the doorway next to a chrome lever that caught Pete's attention.

"What does *that* do?"

"Seriously? It flushes the room, of course."

"Whoaaaaaa," Pete whispered, his eyes darting in thought.

"Go ahead. I can tell you're keen to."

Pete yanked the lever's handle, bringing down a torrent of sudsy water from a sprinkler on the ceiling, thereby soaking both himself and Kyrian.

"Woops," Pete gurgled.

Kyrian pressed a small button next to the lever, and a blast of air filled the room, nearly lifting Pete off his feet. A moment later, the gust subsided, leaving them completely dry.

"And *that's* how you clean the W.C.," Kyrian concluded, walking across the tile floor to knock on the door located at the other end.

"Bennmush, welcome, pinmates," an adenoidal voice said.

Kyrian led the way into the adjoining room, stepping over a half-unpacked footlocker of books. "If it isn't Glenn Simon, as I live and breathe seawater."

Pete followed Kyrian in, doing his best not to step on any of the books strewn on the floor as he faced two thin pasty students slouched in their desk chairs, both wearing thick-framed glasses.

"Felilum to you, Kyrian. I'd like to introduce my Ward, Benn Snodgrass from Dim Delta."

"Two peas in a pod, all right," Kyrian whispered to Pete.

"What is she like?" Benn asked Pete, blinking his eyes behind his high-magnification glasses.

Pete looked to Kyrian for explanation.

"I'm pretty sure he means your mum."

"Oh … uh, you know … she's just Mom," Pete offered weakly.

"I am unclear as to how Aquis was able to acquire this individual from Ignis," Glenn said to Kyrian. "The mathematics suggests it impossible."

"It wasn't easy, Drake being a legacy and all."

"A legacy?" Pete asked.

"It means you're the offspring of someone who was already in that element. And since your mum was in Ignis ..."

"She was in fire? Wow – that's a surprise," Pete said, his mind whirring.

Kyrian regarded Pete with a look of fascination. "How is it you don't know this stuff?"

Glenn looked Pete over and shook his head, his lips pursed. "Most disappointing."

"Agreed," Benn said. "Lacking in both physicality and elementary knowledge."

"And personality," Glenn added.

Hey!

"You do know he's standing right here," Kyrian said.

"We are well aware of his proximity," Glenn said, then held out a sheet of parched seaweed for Kyrian's perusal. "Moving ahead, Benn and I have taken the liberty of drawing up a lavatory schedule."

Kyrian glanced at the schedule then flushed it down the nearest commode. "There will be no need for that, Simon. They just installed four, count 'em, four dunnies in every W.C., remember? Drake, we used to have a real problem with truancy due to digestive issues when there was just one toilet per Pin. The extra ones were added to clear things up, so to speak."

"There remain a variety of other subjects on which we wish to come to terms," Glenn said, adjusting the heavy eyeglasses that kept slipping down his nose. "Music you might play loudly, for one."

Kyrian casually leaned against the wall. "We can listen with earnubs. Next."

"Your voices, should they become loud, for another."

"*You* can wear earnubs."

"Ahem, the rest of the tour, syr?"

Kyrian grinned at the sound of Otto's remonstrance. "Gotta finish our tour. See you boys on the Squallix field." He then put his hand on Pete's shoulder and ushered him back into their own room.

"What does he mean by that?" Benn said, his voice rising with nervousness.

"Here, inhale some oxygen," Glenn said, handing his podmate a squeeze bottle before closing their bathroom door.

"Thanks, Otto. Your timing's impeccable," Kyrian said.

"My manners are impeccable, syr. My timing is precise," Otto corrected.

"Like I said, a pain in the gillbladder," Kyrian joked, then stepped up on his box-stair, preparing to ascend to his hammock.

"So, are you gonna show me more of the Frond?" Pete asked.

Kyrian pivoted on the box and hopped back to the floor. "Fair dinks. Right this way."

Otto held the room's entry door open, and Kyrian sauntered out, sweeping his arm toward the common area where waves of light from an unseen source danced off the walls, furnishings, and aquaria. Each corner of the room featured a fountain in the shape of a legendary aquatic creature, and against the far wall a hot tub bubbled beside a sandpit containing pails and shovels. "This is the Familial Forum, which everyone just calls *the Famm.*"

This is like no family room I've ever seen.

"The main attraction, naturally, is the Galley. We used to have a swim-up food bar, but they moved it over to the semi-submersed Frond while you were going through Appraisement."

Pete was hardly listening. All he could think about was finding which room was Edni's.

Her room's around here somewhere. I can feel it.

"The Caretaker's flat is beside the Galley and, come this way," Kyrian said, walking around a corner. "This is our Blade's study den."

"Sixteen of us share this, right?"

"Yip. It's a good place to get away if your podmate or automaton get too annoying," he said with a grin.

Pete surveyed the room, his mind momentarily off of Edni as he regarded a lamp with a shade made of water on which was projected a scene of swimming sea creatures. A pair of armchairs separated by a table and water lamp occupied each wall. One of the chairs faced into the room. The other faced the wall.

"Interesting set-up with the chairs," Pete remarked.

"Yeah, they do it that way to keep it quiet while Fids study. Doesn't work, of course. And they recently put the fireplace in the center to discourage ball games." Kyrian turned in place to regard the room. "And that's it for the study den." Leading Pete back to the common area, Kyrian pointed to the quarters just beyond their Blade. "Those are the Scions' rooms. Each assistant lives alone in a room the size of our Pod. The lead Scion's room is twice that size! That's where Demo, our Scion, bunks."

"Do you mean that guy Demetrius?"

"Yip. We all call him Demo. You'll meet the A-Scions later."

"A-Scions?"

"Assistants. This sekkl, our Frond's got Brek Crudenski, Mindye Sharpe, and Tat Luvl. Anywaterway, that's the grand tour."

"Do you mind if I wander around a little? Just to get a feel for things?"

"Suit yourself. Nothing much to see."

All I need to see is where Edni lives.

Pete ran a hand over his bangs and tucked his shirt in, his mind working to come up with something clever to say when he saw Edni.

I need to play it cool, relaxed, not come on too strong ... I wonder if it's too soon to ask her to go steady.

{Kapta Fuinenn-Fui}

Chapter Thirty-Three – Holowords

Pete patrolled the hallways, carefully reading the nameplates on every door.

No Edni anywhere.

With a dispirited huff and a pout, he plodded his way back to the podroom, each heavy step feeling as if kettlebells were attached to his ankles.

He opened the door to find Kyrian up in his hammock reading a magazine called *Squallix in Our Time.*

"Hey, Kyrian," he said, doing his best to act casual rather than crushed. "I have a friend in Aquis, but I don't see her name anywhere."

"Must be in the other Frond."

Pete's heart kerplunked.

"What's her name?" Kyrian asked absentmindedly as he turned magazine pages.

"Edni. I don't know if she has a last name … She's an oceanid, if that helps."

Kyrian nodded. "Definitely in the other Frond. That's where they have the underwater rooms. The mers put up a fuss, as usual, and demanded special accommodations."

Pete slumped into his desk chair, self-pity twisting his insides. It was bad enough he'd not been selected to join the domain he wanted—not even by an element from the top half of his preference list—but now, the primary saving grace, Edni, was removed from the equation.

"Perhaps Maistr Peyton would care to freshen up before dressing for the All Ocademy Orientation, syr?" Otto suggested, holding out a fluffy bath sheet bearing the Aquis emblem.

Pete accepted the towel tentatively. "I'm sorry, I have nothing to offer you in the way of a tip."

"A tip? *A tip?!*" the robot fumed, whizzing into the armoire and slamming the door behind him.

Kyrian smirked. "Looks like you just insulted the help."

"No tips. Got it."

Pete headed to the bathroom to drown his woes under a soothing stream of water. As was so often the case, a shower was just the thing he needed to restore his emotional equilibrium.

Maybe I like showers so much cuz I'm an Aquin at heart?

That's what he told himself in an effort to snap out of his funk.

He dressed in white trousers and a V-neck sweater trimmed with blue and green chevron stripes, the Aquis emblem over his heart. Catching sight of Kyrian, he was surprised to find they were clad in the exact same ensemble.

"Oh shoot! We match. Do you want me to change?" Pete asked sheepishly.

"Nopes, and I don't want you to shoot either," Kyrian replied, his hands up in mock surrender. "We're wearing our domain colors. Everyone else will be too."

"Ahem."

Pete looked up to see Otto holding an Aquis-logo necktie in each hand.

"And yeah, we have to wear strangulaters." Kyrian flipped up the collar of his dress shirt to loop, wrap, and tuck the fabric strip into a perfect Windsor knot.

Pete had only worn a tie twice, and both times they were clip-ons. It took him only seconds to knot his tie around his throat and cut off his airflow.

"If Maistr Peyton will allow me, syr," Otto offered.

"Thanks, Otto. I appreciate it," Pete rasped as Otto loosened the knot and reworked Pete's tie.

"That is all the gratuity I require, syr."

"Understood," Pete said with a smile.

Otto opened the door, and Kyrian strode out. "Thanks, Otto. You're a pip."

Pete followed, pulling his hair down over his eyes to hide as he always did at school.

"Walk or slide?" Kyrian asked as they approached the Frond's exit.

"I really want to try the slide, but I think I better use the stairs so I don't mess up my orientation clothes."

"Good call." Kyrian grasped the winding staircase's bannisters and slid his hands down them until he reached the lower level without ever touching a step.

Pete hurried behind him the old-fashioned way, one stair at a time.

They chatted amiably as they moseyed through the glass tunnel leading toward the brink. Seawater ebbed and flowed around the tube, and a variety of the ocean's denizens swam by languidly. Some stopped to look at Pete, unnerving him.

"If we went the other direction, would we end up at the Aquis ocean arena?" Pete asked.

"We sure would. You were there on the playing field during the tsunami, weren't you?"

Pete nodded, shivering at the memory.

"Pretty fun, huh?" Kyrian said, his eyes dancing.

That's one way to put it.

When they got to the brink at the end of the tunnel, Pete pulled up short. Memories of his first encounter with the waterfall entryway flashed through his mind. At the time, he'd been submerged in coal black water with no idea how to escape and only the air in his lungs. He shuddered to think what might have befallen him had a vampire squid not led him to the exit.

"Walk through." Kyrian nudged Pete with his elbow. "Trust me."

Pete took a deep breath and stepped through the waterfall, frantically dog paddling until he realized he was standing in The Hub, his arms thrashing needlessly.

Kyrian exited behind him. "Just shake your head."

Pete did so and was instantly dry—and not in the least bit drowning or dead. "Last time I went through—"

"Last time you went through you didn't have that stamp on your head. Now you're one of us. You can go wherever you need to."

Pete appreciated the logic behind the academy's methods. Try though he might, he could find nothing negative about the academy, his roommate, or even his element domain.

The perimeter of The Hub was lined with tables behind which sat pairs of earnest students touting their cause.

"Welcome to the Club Fair," Kyrian said.

"The Club Fair?"

"Yeah, this is where the specialty groups and factions camp out at the start of the sekkl to nab new members."

"Am I expected to join any of them?"

"Only if you want." Kyrian nodded to the first table they passed. "That's the Show Spectacular group. They're recruiting performers for next sekkl's musical revue."

"The one that took place on my first day of Appraisement?"

"Yip. See this next table? That's for awiding."

"What's awiding?"

"It's when a student spends a sekkl in another realm living with a host family. Most Fids go as a seventh-level."

"Where did you go?"

"I didn't. I chose Squallix over travel. Most people think I made a mistake, but I've got no regrets. I figure I'll get to travel plenty once I'm a voc Squaller. Besides, if I'd gone, I wouldn't be here now and wouldn't be your Warden."

Kyrian grinned and mussed Pete's hair. Pete half-glowered, half-smiled behind his bangs. He hated anyone touching his hair, but he appreciated what Kyrian said.

Raised voices and people hurrying away from two of the fair tables quieted the conversation in The Hub.

"Get your grubby hands off me," snapped a student from Arbis, swatting away a friendly touch from a Platen student.

"Here we go," Kyrian said.

"What's happening?"

"Perennial Sterling and the Pan-Element Fusion are at it again."

"I have no idea what that means."

"Perennial Sterling is a bunch of element elitists who disapprove of relations between members of different elements. The Pan-Element Fusion formed around the time your Mum left the Ocademy. They advocate for interaction and even marriage between the elements. The Perennials detest the Pans."

"They hate them for trying to help people get along?"

"You have to understand, the whole *staying inside your element* thing has been rooted into society for millennia. Old prejudices die hard."

"Have a sunshiny day," a girl said from behind the Song of the Sun table, offering Pete a beaming smile and handing him a cookie in the shape of the sun as he and Kyrian strolled by.

"Those people seem friendly," Pete said, taking a nibble of the cookie.

"That's an understatement. The Beamers are pretty much all smiles and happiness all the time.

"Beamers?"

"Song of the Sun zellies. They've been getting pretty popular the last few seekkl."

"Popular here on campus?"

"Popular everywhere. They're becoming an omniversal movement."

Pete froze on the spot, agog as he looked up a shallow stone stairway at a colossal sphinx lounging on the landing.

Kyrian grinned, slowly backing his way up the stairs. "Say felilum to Sahrlaah, Drake."

"Fay balloon, Sarla," he squeaked.

The great beast replied with a lazy roar that sent a gust of wind whistling through The Hub.

"Looks like she approves of you," Kyrian said, gamboling past the sphinx. "...Today, Fiddlehead!" he called back to Pete.

Pete summoned his courage and ran as fast as he could without daring a glance at the giant feline. When he got to where Kyrian stood waiting, he found himself facing a pair of gold-horned unicorns.

"Go ahead, pull one," Kyrian said.

"You must be joking," Pete replied.

Pete had always been anxious around animals and unsure how to behave when near them. His father had never allowed the family to have pets, aside from a singular purchase of sea monkeys that lived out their brief lives in one of Cassie's casserole dishes. The lieutenant didn't even allow Pete to play with the next door neighbor's puppy, referring to it as *a flea-bitten crone* and chasing it off with a push broom whenever it stepped onto the Drake's lawn.

"No need to be a timid tuna," Kyrian said, running his hand down the back of the unicorn nearest him then gently grabbing its golden spike and pulling it toward him.

The unicorn slowly advanced, the door behind it opening in sync with the unicorn's steps.

"Hurry up, squib. Sentients are waiting!" someone behind Pete shouted.

Pete only got as far as placing a forefinger on the other unicorn's horn before scurrying into the room where he froze in his tracks yet again, this time at the sight of the nonuple-story hall—a space more grandiose than any of the academy areas he'd visited thus far.

"What is this place?" he whispered, his eyes boggling.

"It's where we eat. It's the only place on campus where everyone comes together."

"That's like at home—we only all get together for meals."

Kyrian pointed overhead to a selection of rugs floating around the perimeter. "Any guess what those are for?"

"For the people from Nitris?"

Kyrian smiled. "You're a quick learner. That's good. Sheffield says humility and the willingness to learn are key to success, on and off the field.

"Who?"

"Hey, I see Demo. Let's grab seats by him before this place goes nutty."

Pete mindlessly followed, still drinking in the grandeur of the resplendent hall. Like many of the spaces at the academy, the room was round with a domed ceiling that resembled the sky—in this case, with the addition of a brilliant sun shining straight overhead. A series of mahogany Corinthian columns ornamented with brass capitals supported the structure, uninterrupted except for a balcony high above the dining floor.

Polished wood paneling ran around the room's long circular wall up to waist high, capped by wainscoting. The upper portion of the ground floor wall was composed of etched frosted glass, as was the balcony's wall. Separating the balcony from the sky was crown molding studded with brass rosettes. More than once Pete bumped into someone while admiring the overhead décor as he walked.

Carved sideboards sat at intervals against the curved wall, each outfitted with a set of three samovars, along with a variety of cups, mugs, and glasses. Pete hoped at least one of the urns held a cache of Barely Berry Whizbang Punch—or tea. The twelve-dozen dining tables were bedecked with silver and crystal epergnes bearing exotic fruits, a special touch reserved for the first all-academy meal.

Domains and cliques claimed their turf straight off with students using their sweaters, neckties, and even shoes to save seats for their comrades. The more traditional students preferred to dine from the chaises and footed trays that rimmed the block of dining tables. Pete noticed his pinmates, Glenn and Benn, occupying two adjoining chaises, the two boys' small frames making them look like children on the elegant divans.

The capacious room was packed to capacity, but unlike the kerfuffle that took place in the Crux on Druthers Day, the company was restrained and well-behaved.

Kyrian and Pete squeezed onto a bench with several Aquins whom Kyrian quickly introduced to Pete. Pete recognized some of the Aquins from the midnight feast on the barge, but his mind was so full, he felt certain he would forget everyone's names by the time the meal was served. He feared he just might forget his own!

A hush fell over the room as Curator Theod's tiny swirl of sparks drifted into the space. Once the Curator fully materialized, he floated for several seconds, smiling wordlessly, his lavender hair flowing in six long braids reaching down to the hem of his kilt.

"Vilranyuh, vilranyuh dut," he said, clapping his hands to his chest.

Several students nodded sagely.

Pete looked at Kyrian.

"He just thanked us."

Pete couldn't imagine why. Surely, he for one had not done anything worthy of the headmaster's thanks. As the Curator launched into a disquisition about the history of the academy and his esteem for its staff and students, Pete scoured the section of tables commandeered by the Aquins. At last he located Edni who he believed looked nothing short of radiant in her simple sweater and pleated skirt. He tried to catch her eye, but to no avail. All eyes except his were on the Curator. Kyrian pinched him to get him to pay attention.

When the audience applauded, Pete realized he'd ignored the entire speech, and he fretted he'd missed some vital piece of information that would later save his life.

The Curator bowed humbly and concluded. "And now, we have a short holovid we'd like to share with you, prepared over the twixt-term hiatus."

The gas lamps on the mahogany columns dimmed as the Curator shrunk down to a small swirl. A cheesy pop song played, and from behind the great hall's columns, holographic shapes of the six estates' twelve Caretakers danced and sang their way toward the center of the room, each wearing a silly mask and colorful robe. When the shapes converged and the song ended, a flash of light eclipsed the room. The audience clapped in appreciation.

The Caretakers squinted anxiously at one another through the brightness. The recording crackled and popped, and in its place a single form appeared wearing a black cloak that looked to be made of dragon scales. Obscuring his face was a pewter mask that looked like a Viking shield with the Omni logo at its center.

Several in the crowd murmured, "It's XQ."

A strange and disquieting tune played as a second shape, dressed identically, emerged from behind the first and stood beside it. The sequence repeated until six holographic figures stood back-to-back in a circle, hovering over the dining floor.

The older students whispered to one another, their expressions worried.

The first figure spoke in a digitally-disguised voice as his companions hummed an unsettling melody. "How many more lives will you lose to Oblivion before you are willing to cast aside your lies and shadows? We are Exaequos, and we are here to wield the sword of truth to hack away the corruption of Axis's decaying dictatorial rule. Take the power back from the oligarchs and return it into the hands of the dimensions. Join our crusade for freedom, or see your world turned into a battlefield."

"We're not afraid of you!" Demetrius shouted, his clarion voice ringing through the hall.

Pete was astounded. The thought Demetrius would stand up to the despots instead of laying low until they went away was incomprehensible to Pete.

Demetrius stepped atop the dining table and stared in defiance at the hologram. "And we're not falling for your fearmongering."

Pete's pancreas folded in on itself.

"Then we haven't been doing our jobs correctly," the figure taunted.

Another burst of blinding light crackled through the hall. The Wardens of younger students directed their Wards to seek safety beneath the tables.

"Get behind me," Kyrian said in a low voice, surreptitiously pulling Pete's arm to change places with him and shield him.

Demetrius continued, standing only a few feet away from Pete. "There's no need for a coup or whatever scheme you have planned. The Omniversical Council has kept peace within the dimensions since the Magno Silentium of 1213 R.C."

"You dare to speak of peace and The Great Hush? A conspiracy of rule by fear. Harmony is a myth."

"If that's the case, why are people flocking to the Song of the Sun, a movement that advocates peace and unity."

"Your naiveté is matched only by your hubris. What is your name, foolish boy?"

"I am Demetrius Girard Theodocious Nickleby!"

Muted gasps sucked the air out of the room.

"Good going, Demo, now they know who you are," Kyrian said under his breath, hanging his head and shaking it in concern.

"The Curator's son, how very propitious," said the cloaked hologram figure. "Tell me, what do you believe you alone can do compared to all of XQ?"

"He's not alone!" a tenth-level girl from Nitris cried, climbing onto her dining table.

A scattering of older students followed suit, joining in solidarity with Demetrius.

"Stay low and don't move," Kyrian whispered to Pete before stepping up onto the table with the elder Aquins.

"Sit down, children," the hologram figure said, his tone mocking.

Demetrius clenched his fists. "Not without a fight."

"Very well. A fight you shall have." The figure twirled, as did the five other hologram shapes, fading into nothingness.

The room went still except for a buzz of electrostatic and the sounds of whimpering coming from beneath several of the tables.

"Anything?" the Curator asked, materializing. "Did I allow them to spew their drivel long enough for you to track their broadcast hub?"

"No, syr," a disembodied voice said. "They jammed our sub-frequency. We couldn't get a reading."

"Thrash it all!" the Curator said. "Omnians, as you can see, the rebel threat is real, make no mistake. Scion Demetrius, you are the reason we refer to Ocademy students as Fiddleheads. What in Tohubohu were you thinking? That impetuous stunt of yours was exceptionally dangerous – and exceptionally courageous. I, for one, would be proud to have a son like you … Oh wait …"

A collective chuckle reduced the tension in the room. Pete sat silent, too unnerved to even assault his cuticles.

"All clear, syr," the disembodied voice announced. "We've done a synchronous sweep and double-checked all the portal gauges. No signs of intrusion or foreign bodies."

"Curious … Very good, thank you, Reig." The Curator smiled at the crowd. "I don't know about you all, but anarchy really whets my appetite."

Chuckling again, the older students easily fell back into their previous conversations. The bulk of the new pupils gradually regained their sangfroid and joined in socializing. A few, like Pete, remained aghast.

Curator Theod clapped three times then waved his hands over his head, calling down strands of pasta from on high, the whimsical delivery of lunch effectually putting Pete and the last of the worried greenhorns at ease. Diners scrambled to collect plates from tray jacks and pass the crockery to their tablemates. Kyrian grabbed a pair of silver scissors from the nearest epergne and cut the pasta thread piling onto his plate, curtailing its flow. He then handed the scissors to Pete as casually as if he were passing the saltshaker.

A troop of service gnomes on roller skates sped past, sending bowls of salad, meat sauce, and Parmesan cream sauce sliding down each table. From the balcony, a band of gnomes dressed in track-and-field gear launched javelin-like bread baguettes over the crowd as students playfully grappled with one another to catch the incoming loaves.

"Meals sure aren't fun like this back home," Pete remarked to Kyrian, using a chunk of bread to sop up the meat sauce.

"Eat fast," he whispered in response.

Pete was afraid to ask why and kept an eye out for anyone in a black dragon scale cloak or Viking mask as he devoured his food.

The moment their bowls were empty, Pete heard a whizzing sound heading in their direction. He ducked, fearing a rebel missile attack. Kyrian tapped Pete's shoulder and pointed to the balcony where a pack of gnomes with binoculars strapped to their faces held slingshots, grinning mischievously. A thud and clatter drew Pete's attention to his bread plate where he found a scoop of spumoni.

"Well that looks unappetizing," Pete said, pushing the plate of muted-hued ice cream aside.

"Maybe, but it tathes delithiouth," Kyrian replied, the cold of the sub-zero ice cream rendering speech difficult. "Now, rattle your dagth."

"Huh?"

"At leatht try thome, and hurry!"

Pete swiped his forefinger across the blob of ice cream and dabbed it on the tip of his tongue. He then dug his spoon in and took a large bite, eliciting a smile of approval from Kyrian. Pete considered asking what the rush was about, but the spumoni made his mouth too cold to form words. He quickly finished his dessert and turned to catch Kyrian licking his own plate.

"Oh, you're done," Kyrian said, flushing at being caught lapping up the spumoni remnants. "Alley-oop then."

They gathered their dirty dishes and speed-walked toward the entry doors, hastily depositing their things in various designated bins.

"Hand me your materials list," Kyrian said.

"I don't have it," Pete replied in contrition.

"Sure ya do. I put my Warden's copy in your strides pocket when you were showering."

"Strides?" he said, stopping to look at his feet.

Kyrian waved a finger at Pete's legs. "Your dacks ... tweeds ... trousers ... *pants*?"

Pete reached into both pockets and detected the folded paper, removing it and passing it to Kyrian who read it as they turned down one of the shop walkways.

"I think my uniform might be ready," Pete mentioned as they passed Habitual Habiliments and Haberdashery.

"Our valet probably already picked it up. We need to get the other stuff, fast."

"What's the hurry?" Pete finally asked.

"About an hour from now every shop in The Hub will be wall-to-wall with Fids shopping for supplies, but we're gonna beat them to it."

"Very shrewd," Pete said, quickening his pace.

"We'll start at Volumes and Verses. The Preceptors will let you slide a lum or two without all your gear, but you don't wanna start class without your books or you'll fall behind from the jump." Kyrian stopped in front of the bookstore and peered through the paned glass window. "Bonzers, the place looks empty. All right then, let's get to it. The History and Cosmology section's right over there. You grab *Antediluvian Chronicling* – make sure it's the one for Troglodytes. Also pick up *Flenning's,* and the *Cyclopedia Omniverica*. I'll fetch the rest and meet you at the counter."

Pete quickly located the three books, but was hard-pressed to carry them all. The big and boxy Flenning's volume was fairly manageable. *Antediluvian Chronicling,* however, kept verbally insulting him and snapped its metal cover shut on his fingers whenever he tried to pick it up. The *Cyclopedia Omniverica* was docile enough, but its globe shape was problematic. Pete identified no clear method of closing or even reading the book. Plus, it kept rolling away.

Kyrian and Pete approached the counter at the same time, both failing to hang on to their books.

A friendly shop girl with butterflies circling her head greeted them. "Felilum, Fids! Find everything you need, want, and desire?"

Pete looked to Kyrian who said, "Yes, ma'arm."

"How corking," the girl replied.

"We're ready to purchase," Kyrian added.

"Ooooooh so exciting, isn't it?" she tittered.

"If you could ring us up …"

"Wish I could. I'm just the help desk." She pointed to a counter across the shop. "But the checkers right over there should have you taken care of in a spiff."

Pete tucked the round tome under his chin and followed Kyrian to the checkout desk where they encountered a line of four people.

"Doesn't look too bad," Pete said.

Kyrian smirked in satisfaction as he casually took a place behind the fourth person in line. "What did I tell ya? Beat 'em to the punch."

"Excuse me," said a tiny voice.

Pete turned around, but couldn't find who was speaking.

"I'm right here," the voice said.

Pete stepped sideways and noticed a faerie standing around the corner. Behind her waited the rest of the serpentine queue, extending farther than the eye could see.

"Umm, Kyrian?" Pete said, nodding to the rest of the line.

Kyrian peered around the corner, took one look at the queue, and dropped his mountain of books on his foot.

{Kapta Fuinenn-Ud}

CHAPTER THIRTY-FOUR – DRUDGERY & DUTY

Three hours after joining the bookstore queue, the podmates trudged back through the Aquis brink dragging heavy burlap sacks behind them. Kyrian was still limping when they arrived at the base of the corkscrew staircase, his foot aching from the load of books that crashed down on it.

"How are we going to—" Pete began.

"We're not," Kyrian said, leaving his bag of books with Pete and hobbling up the steps.

"I really wish this place had an elevator," Pete said under his breath, stumped as to how to get the books up the stairs.

"Here," Kyrian said, lowering his torso halfway down the slide. "Push them up to me and I'll pull them the rest of the way."

Pete toiled to shove each bag up without having it slide back down before Kyrian could reach it. After a few unsuccessful attempts, the plan worked, and Pete and Kyrian were back in their room, both lying flat on the floor after the tedium of waiting in line.

"Right then, what's next on your skej?" Kyrian asked, massaging his foot.

Pete rolled over and reached up onto his chair where his welcome circular lay. "Looks like we're supposed to meet our pinmates."

"Already did that, thank the Aethereans."

"The Aethereans?" Pete said, thinking of Esperança and missing their talks.

"It's just an expression. The Aethereans are always off doing good things in secret, so when something goes unexpectedly good ..."

"You thank the Aethereans."

Kyrian touched his forefinger to his nose.

"So we can check that off the list," Pete said. "After that, we're supposed to meet with our blademates in the study den for a *hospitality reception and Sups.*"

Kyrian groaned. "Ugh, it takes forever and is more boring than watching coral grow, but it's something we *have to* do. It would be disrespectful not to. Mana, respect, is a big thing at the Ocademy. That's why there are so few violent incidents here ... Well, unless you count the recent rebel stuff."

Pete struggled not to guffaw. In his eyes, *rebel stuff* counted to the nth degree. He changed the subject to keep the memory of the XQ holograms from consuming his thoughts. "It says it's a repast, so at least we get food, right?"

"Not until after – to keep Fids from grubbing and bolting. They hold us hostage with the lure of Cookie's cooking. Sadists! What's after we nosh?"

"Oh uhh, it says my Warden is supposed to take me on a *leisurely stroll through the Illumination level to familiarize me with the fruit sectors and my class locations.* What's with all the fruit names?"

Kyrian groaned again. "It's a pointlessly protracted and absurd story."

Pete sat up, smiling eagerly. Long stories were generally his favorite stories. The addition of absurdity made it all the more enticing.

"Okay, here goes," Kyrian began. "Around the time the Pan-Element Fusion was formed – during the era when everyone was into breaking down social barriers and promoting concord – a group of tight-wound Ocademy empaths complained that the areas on the Illumination level were named after the elements located above them."

Pete shrugged, not grasping the problem.

"My thoughts exactly," Kyrian said. "But the empaths said the practice was prejudicial for reasons sane people have never understood. So, the Bureau administrators in office at the time renamed the areas using numbers. But the empaths whinged about that too, nagging that the numbers made it seem like some sections were better than others. Then the Bureau tried letters—"

"I see where this is going."

"Yip, the empaths bellyached again, claiming the letters at the beginning of the alphabet got top billing. Finally, the Bureau threw up their hands and assigned the sections fruit names according to the Swizzle-Burman Six-Color Wheel to keep things organized. No one can say the Bureau isn't organized."

"You're right. That story was totally absurd."

The podmates chuckled together, and Pete became conscious of a connection he'd not felt in years—friendship. Aside from his mother, he had no one at home he could talk to so comfortably. Engaging in conversation with his father was usually an exercise in tongue-biting and regret. Trying to talk to his younger brother, Billy, was even less pleasant and usually resulted in Pete walking away with bruised flesh. Owing to Lt. Drake's five-year ban on Pete fraternizing with schoolmates, Pete couldn't remember the last time he had a pal with whom he could shoot the breeze.

"Is that the last thing on your itinerary then?" Kyrian asked.

"Huh? Oh, umm there's a themed dessert social here in our Familial Forum, hosted by our Galleymaster."

"That's another thing we can't miss, not so much out of respect, but cuz Cookie mixes a mean egg cream."

"One thing I'll say for this place, they sure have good food."

"Enjoy it while you can. Once you're deep into your classes and Squallix practice, food will be the last thing on your mind."

Pete's pancreas cramped.

Why did he have to go and spoil everything by bringing up sports?!

"Ahem," Otto said, emerging from the armoire.

"That time already?" Kyrian asked, lethargically getting up from the floor.

"It is indeed, syr."

Kyrian pulled off his Aquis sweater and lobbed it on his desk chair. "We won't need to wear our colors anymore tonight. It's all in-house hobnobbing from here on out."

Pete removed his sweater and folded it before placing it on his chair.

"Time to face the Fids," Kyrian said, lacing his fingers and stretching his arms out in front of him.

"Bye, Otto. We'll just be next door if you need us," Pete said.

"Very good, syr."

Kyrian chuckled. "Alley-oop, Q boy. Let's go talk to some beings with pulses."

🦅🦅🦅

They arrived in the study den to find Glenn and Benn already there, both still wearing their Aquis sweaters.

"Felilum, pins," Kyrian said, turning all of the chairs facing the walls inward toward the fireplace.

"Mind if I join you?" a friendly voice asked from behind them.

Pete turned to find Demetrius obscuring the doorway. Pete had never been so close to him and was awestruck by the elder student's size and demeanor. Kyrian looked like a mere boy compared to the force of nature that was Demetrius. Pete felt like a toddler.

"Feel free," Glenn answered Demetrius dispassionately, seemingly impervious to Demetrius' formidability.

Kyrian turned the last of the armchairs around and jumped over the back of one, landing in a seated position in the center of it. "What's quakin', Demo?"

"You tell me, Kyrs." Demetrius nodded toward Pete. "I see you have a new Ward."

"That sure was valiant of you today, Mr. Demetrius, standing up to the rebels like that," Pete gushed, immediately wishing he could crawl in a hole and hide in embarrassment.

Demetrius smiled at him. "Valiant – I like that. Thanks, Drake!"

Pete nodded, astonished that someone like Demetrius the Valiant would speak to a gnat like himself, let alone know his name.

"Kyrs, let's get some more seats in here, eh?" Demetrius walked out the door, trailed by Kyrian. "That means you too, Drake."

Pete scuttled to follow.

Kyrian opened a closet in the Famm and pulled out nine colorful rubber cubes, each about a foot square. He gave three to Demetrius who handed them to Pete, then Demetrius and Kyrian took the rest and returned to the study den.

"Ready?" Demetrius said with a grin, standing over one of the cubes, his fist poised in the air above it.

Kyrian nodded, also standing over a cube. They each brought their fist down hard onto the rubber. Instantly, two bouncy armchairs popped into shape.

"Your turn, Drake," Demetrius said.

Pete steadied himself over a pink cube and struck with all his might. The rubber repelled his blow, sending him stumbling into a wall. Kyrian and Demetrius let out a hearty laugh. To Pete, the situation was no laughing matter, but a challenge he was determined to tackle. The last thing he wanted to do was look as wimpy as he felt.

Demetrius' arm is about as big as my whole body, how am I supposed to ... That's it!

41

Pete pushed away the hair covering his eyes and took a running leap, landing in the center of the cube and causing it to pop open fully.

"Nice work, Drake!" Demetrius said, snapping in recognition.

Yeaaaa!

"Can't wait to see what you do on the Squallix field," he added.

Booooo!

As the room gradually filled with the remaining members of the sixteen-student Blade, Demetrius pushed a button that retracted the fireplace up into the ceiling. "Now we can all see one another," he said, smiling genially.

Glenn pursed his lips in disapproval. "They installed that fireplace to keep people from playing ball in the study dens."

"Then, Simon, I suggest you not *play ball* during our Nod'n'Nosh," Demetrius replied with a good-humored grin.

Pete hung on his every word.

Demetrius continued. "Let's go around the room and introduce ourselves. After all, we're gonna be seeing a whole lot of each other."

The students sized up one another with a mixture of curiosity and mild annoyance.

Kyrian slid down in his seat and whispered to Pete. "Wake me up when it's over."

"Please state your name, level, and whether you're new here," Demetrius instructed, "as well as where you're from, and something about you … your favorite hobby, for example."

No one said a word.

"All right, I guess I'll start. My name's Demetrius Nickleby. I usually don't let on that I'm the Curator's son, but I guess that secret went out the window at Ocademy orientation. I'm a ninth-level, born right here on campus, so I don't actually have a home planet or dimension."

A couple of the girls *awwed* in sympathy.

"To help me feel more rooted, Pops used to tell me I was ultra fortunate – cuz I was a child of the Omniverse as a whole, not just one place. Before Pops became a Preceptor, he and my mum lived in Dim Omega on a planet called Sparga in the Surging Sea galactic cluster. I'm an avid Squaller, and really excited to be promoted to full Scion this sekkl … and I've said more than I intended."

He smiled at the student next to him. She licked her lips, inhaled deeply, and weakly began. "My name is Iyoma Baeg. I'm from Dim H, which we like to say is the Howdy Dimension." She smiled faintly. "My home planet of Fenn was blown up in the Colossal Misunderstanding. I'm a new fifth-level. My favorite pastime is to observe. I do a lot of bird and bug watching back at home … Well, at my cousin's home now that mine's gone." She sighed, turning increasingly mawkish.

Demetrius put a comforting hand on her shoulder. "Maybe we should skip the part about our home planets," he said compassionately. Iyoma looked up into his face and sniffled, her eyes welling and lower lip trembling. "Who's next?" he asked.

Pete struggled to stay alert as several new students and their Wardens introduced themselves.

"Bam!" a feisty girl said, rousing everyone. "That's what people call me – short for Alibammer, but Bam suits me better. I'm a first-sekkl fourth-level from Dim Zeta and a hard-to-the-core Pachinko competitor. I'll be representing my dimension in next sekkl's Galilean Games."

"She's got all the makings of a brute," Kyrian confided to Pete.

Pete was appalled by the insult, unaware that *brute* was a term for a Squallix player and thus, high praise coming from Kyrian.

A few moments later, with eyes closed, Kyrian mumbled, "Nine."

He must be talking in his sleep … or in German.

43

"Felilum, good to see ya," a clean-cut high-energy male said, striding around the room shaking hands. "Pax is the name, and politics is my ticket to fame. I'm a sixth-level from Dim S. Yes, I think government is super, and you can count on me to clean it up. I'm applying to be the Fiddlehead Bureau Liaison. It's a volunteer position, but here, take a campaign button anyway. Friends, a vote for Pax is a—"

"Pax buddy," Demetrius interjected, "how about you hold off barnstorming 'til we get through the rest of the Blade intros, eh?"

Pax returned to his seat silently, wilting, his head hanging.

"Don't feel glum," Demetrius added. "You'll have an audience four times this size at the Sarsaparilla Social later this shad. I hope you've got plenty of buttons to hand out!"

Pax smiled and nodded with enthusiasm.

Demetrius turned his attention to Glenn. "Simon, the floor is yours."

"Felilum, fellow Fiddleheads. I am Glenn Simon, a ninth-level from Dim T. I am a multi-medal-winning cerebral gymnast and am renowned for my ability to tolerate lesser beings."

Kyrian hissed quietly for Pete's amusement.

"And now, I surrender the floor to my Ward, Benn Snodgrass."

"My name is Benn Snodgrass. I am a first-sekkl and fifth-level. I am from Dim Delta. My career goal is to create a pocket universe. My current objective is to emulate my exemplary Warden, Glenn Simon."

"Twelve," Kyrian said under his breath, exhaling and shifting in his seat.

Ohhhh he's counting the number of introductions.

"Only four to go," Pete whispered to Kyrian.

Kyrian smiled, his eyes still closed.

It finally dawned on Pete that he too would have to introduce himself, and he couldn't think of anything that would be interesting enough to say.

"Drake," Demetrius said. "… Uh, Drake? … Hello …"

Still feigning sleep, Kyrian kicked Pete to get his attention.

"Huh? Oh is it my turn?"

"For a few teekk more, yes," Demetrius teased.

"Oh ... okay ... well ... How's it going?"

"That's awfully personal," a girl said sternly, folding her arms and turning away.

"Oh, umm, I just meant how are you all doing?"

"How are we doing *what*, precisely?" Benn asked.

"Is there something wrong with Drake?" Pax whispered to Kyrian.

Kyrian responded by kicking him too.

"Umm, I just got here," Pete said. "I'm a fourth-level. At least I think I am. I come from Dimension Q – or so I've been told," he added with a nervous chuckle. No one picked up on his humor. He cleared his throat and continued. "Anyway, my name's Pete, uh, Peyton Drake, and what I most like to do is—"

"No way that's Cassiopeia Salvatori's son," an older student said, eyeing Pete skeptically.

Benn chimed in. "My thoughts exactly. He's not remotely—"

Kyrian interrupted. "Drake here is my Ward and he's a good Fid. Anything you wanna say about him you can say to me. Clear? ... Sorry to interrupt you, Pete."

"No, that's okay. I was done," Pete said, hiding behind his bangs.

"Looks like you're up, Kyrs," Demetrius said.

"Fair enough. I'm Kyrian Parata, a seventh-level from Dim Theta. As for hobbies, I'd cite Squallix, but that's really more of a way of life for me. It's my one true love."

Iyoma sighed and fluttered her eyelashes at Kyrian.

He carried on, unfazed. "If a career in sports doesn't work out, I reckon I'll go into something more stable and mundane like becoming a teatricor."

"What's that?" Iyoma asked, nearly swooning.

"What some dimensions call an *actor* … Can we grub now, Demo?"

"Absolutely! Hule huli, Fiddleheads! You made it through the Nod'n'Nosh!" Demetrius opened the door and let out a trilling whistle. "Aquins, please welcome our Galleymaster, Belinda Cookie Koch. She's someone else you'll be seeing a lot of, luckily for you."

"Oh, stop," the apple-cheeked woman said, carrying a covered tray nearly as large as her arm-span.

"You're all in for a treat," Demetrius said, stepping aside to allow Cookie to pass. "Cookie's made us a traditional oceanic dish that is said to have magical properties."

"Consarn it!" Cookie said. "The tray won't fit through the doorway."

Demetrius and Kyrian looked at each other, both wearing mischievous grins.

"Sure it will," Demetrius said, taking the tray from her. "You may want to stand back, Cookie."

The two sportsmen stood on either side of the doorway—one outside, one inside. Kyrian pulled the tray while Demetrius pushed it, both tipping it this way and that.

"I can't watch," Cookie said, peering between her fingers.

"Drake, table!" Demetrius called out, leaning a massive shoulder against the tray and forcing it through the doorway.

Pete dragged one of the study den's tiny end tables to the center of the room. It took all four tables to come up with a surface large enough to bear the tray.

Cookie bumbled in with a stack of plates and napkins nearly tumbling out of her grasp. Pete relieved her of them and distributed them. It felt good to help out, even if only in small ways, and he appreciated how Demetrius and Kyrian included him. He could have sworn he'd grown an inch in height throughout the day, but dared not look at his reflection. He was on a high and wanted to stay there.

"Ready to do the honors, Cookie?" Demetrius asked, gesturing toward the covered tray.

Pete nearly salivated at the prospect of the delicacies hidden under the tray's lid.

Cookie grinned and lifted the lid. "Wiksto!"

The blademates *ooohed*.

Pete eyed the viands and frowned in disappointed incredulity. "Sandwiches? ... Seriously?"

"You've heard of them?" Kyrian said. "Bilmin fintastic, aren't they?"

"Umm ..."

"Try this," Kyrian said, holding a sandwich under Pete's nose. "It's one of my faves. You'll never guess what it is."

"Tunafish?"

"Jasper's clogs! How did you know that?"

"Cuz we have sandwiches where I come from too," Pete said, dropping onto his plate an egg salad on rye and a turkey on wheat.

"But how do you know about sand-witches? You live on land, not down in the sea."

"Cuz the sandwich is named after a guy who lived on land on my planet a few hundred years ago, the Earl of Sandwich."

Kyrian nearly spit out his food. "Who shoveled you that load of barnacles? These little bread beauties were invented whillions of seekkl ago by a sand witch named Sanndi Eilunnd in Dim Psi. That's why they're called sand-witches!"

Pete looked at him, dumfounded. Wishing to avoid disputation with his affable podmate, Pete elected to go the diplomatic route. "Well, wherever they came from, they sure are tasty."

"That's because where they *came from* is Cookie's Galley," Demetrius interposed.

"I'll second that," Kyrian said, gobbling down two roast beef sandwiches. "Hold on! I bet I know something you've never had before, Drake. You're sure to go potty over it. Stay here!"

A moment later, Kyrian returned with a goofy smile and his hands behind his back. "Close your eyes. This will knock your comet's tail out of orbit. It's a Cookie specialty."

Pete closed his eyes, tingling in anticipation of the splendiferous creation that awaited him.

"You can open them now."

Pete lifted his eyelids to find an oozing sandwich an inch from his nose. "It's a P.B.J. … on Wonder bread."

Kyrian gasped. "Come again?"

"It's peanut butter and jelly with white bread. My mom makes those for me pretty much every other day."

"You're joking, right? He's joking, right, Cookie?"

The Galleymaster shrugged and wiped the crumbs off the tables.

"I have no words," Kyrian lamented.

Pete put out a finger to catch a drip of jelly before it escaped. "Concord grape."

Kyrian took a long look at the forlorn sandwich then crammed it into his mouth. "Wanna go check out where your classes are?" he sputtered. "If we go now, we'll best the crush."

Pete nodded, eager to avoid the crowds they faced when buying textbooks.

"We're gonna slip down to Illumo," Kyrian whispered to Demetrius, referring to the Illumination Strata of the campus where the classrooms and library were located.

"Good plan."

"Slide or stairs?" Kyrian asked as he and Pete snuck out of the room and dashed toward the estate exit.

"Slide, please. And do you think we can maybe stop at Connie's at the carousel for some ice cream?"

"We just noshed a heap of sandos!"

Pete shrugged, having been less than enthused by the sandwich offerings.

"Wait for the Sarsaparilla Social. It'll be worth it. Trust me."

Pete yawned. While he was too worn out to do any more socializing—having had little sleep the night before—he very much liked the idea of a dessert party. He yawned again, unable to help himself.

"I know you're knackered, but not to worry. Illumo is sure to be dead empty just now. We'll pop round your classrooms and be back in the Famm before you can say, 'Bob's your uncle.'"

Pete couldn't fathom why anyone would say *Bob's your uncle*, but at the moment he didn't care. He just wanted to get this last errand of the night over with then cap off the evening with a root beer float before turning in for a full night's sleep.

"You've got a more intense day ahead tomorrow than most," Kyrian said, "what with being new to ... well ... *everything!* That's why I'm taking you to Illumo now when it's quiet, to ensure you face zero stress."

{Kapta Fuinenn-Jai}

Chapter Thirty-Five – Belly on up to the Bar

Following their slide and waterfall departure, Kyrian led Pete down a narrow walkway off The Hub and paused at the foot of a pristinely maintained escalator with high-polish wooden handrails, corrugated glass sides, and filigree steel steps.

"I thought the classrooms were downstairs. This escalator's going up," Pete said.

"Nadalien's going wherever we need her to," Kyrian said.

"Nadalien?"

"Long time no ride, Kyrian," a seductive female voice purred. "Your timing couldn't be better. I'm just coming off my union break."

"Nice sheen," Kyrian said, stepping onto the conveyant and stroking the handrail. "Looks like you were getting some pampering over the break."

"You like it?" the voice asked.

Pete realized it was the escalator that was speaking.

"I went with a red chestnut stain this time," the voice continued. "I was hoping you'd notice."

"How could I not?" Kyrian replied. "You look beautiful, Nadalien."

"That makes two of us," Nadalien said. "Who's the accessory?"

"My new podmate, Peyton – from Dim Q."

"Dim Q? Sounds like you've got your work cut out for you."

"Nah, he's no trouble. And if he acts up, I'll have you take him down to the oubliette."

"Oubliette?" Pete asked.

"The torture chamber," Kyrian explained.

"The academy has a torture chamber?!" Pete yelped.

"So, which way, boys?" Nadalien asked.

Kyrian nudged Pete.

"Umm, the Illumination level, if you please, ma'am," Pete said loudly, unsure where to direct his comment.

"My pleasure," the escalator said, collapsing its steps and sinking down below floor level. "Illumination Strata – going down – The Wheel, classrooms, Athenaeum, observatory," she drawled.

A swarm of students crowded on behind them as they descended to confront a scene of choking chaos. The Wheel (the spoked space connecting the classroom sectors) was clogged with students all unsuccessfully trying to travel in opposing directions. Kyrian and Pete stood inert for several seconds, unable to exit the escalator as scores of students rushed onto it from below. Kyrian went over the side of the escalator's bannister, only succeeding in stepping on someone's head before vaulting back over onto the escalator steps.

It didn't take long before Pete became claustrophobic and Kyrian's patience ran out.

"This is your idea of zero stress?" Pete squawked.

"I've never seen anything like the masses today," Kyrian said. "Then again, we've never replaced half the student body in a single go. We'll never get through all this."

"What are we gonna do?"

"Nadalien?"

"Yes, handsome?" she cooed.

"If anyone asks, you're out of order – at least for the next five omaa. That all right with you?"

"I'll say. My joints are killing me."

Kyrian clasped his hands behind the small of his back and instructed Pete. "Climb up."

"Do what?!"

"On my shoulders. It's the only way. Quick, before everyone does it."

🦅🦅🦅

Ten minutes later, they bounded up Aquis' corkscrew staircase, laughing joyously.

"That was far out!" Pete said as they fell into a pair of the Famm's water-filled armchairs.

"Far out? More like far too close. There was no way in Tohubohu we could've waded through that quag."

"Well it worked great. In fact, I probably had a better view from your shoulders than I would've on the ground. Although I don't get why the administration didn't put class location maps in our welcome circulars. Actually, it would be really helpful to have a map of the whole school."

"Just as well these days. Imagine if the rebels had the schematics to the Ocademy. When I first got here, they used to give us maps and make us memorize them then eat them so they wouldn't leave campus. Nasty buggers. *Bleckh*."

"So why'd they stop? Cuz the maps tasted bad?"

"No. It was cuz Fids kept forgetting to destroy them and maps ended up all over the Omniverse. Parents and rellies started breaching protocols and dropping in at all hours. It got so out of hand the Bureau threatened to move the entire campus again."

"Again?"

"The old campus was around for like forty-nine hundred seekkl. It's said to have been one of the eleven wonders of the Omniverse."

"Why'd they move it the first time?"

52

"It was when the Bureau finally decided to let Platen in as an element and had to redesign the school's layout to make room for them. It was a really big deal at the time. Lots of committee meetings and a little bloodshed, so I've heard."

"This place is crazy! Nothing like the world I come from. What's your world like?"

Benn and Glenn approached, sitting on a watercouch in unison and blinking at Pete and Kyrian.

"A story for another time," Kyrian told Pete.

The Frond's remaining students filed into the Famm in relative silence. All were exhausted from the Appraisement Cycle rush, and the new Fiddleheads were visibly nervous about their impending first day of class.

"Step raht up buckaroos 'n' git yer sasperilly," Cookie called from behind the Galley counter, a ten-gallon cowboy hat on her head and bandana around her neck.

Pete couldn't suppress a chortle.

"Cookie, tell Drake here where you went awiding and served your post-academy outernship," Kyrian called.

The Galleymaster crooked her thumbs through the belt-loops on her blue jeans and stepped out from behind the counter, a pair of spurs jangling as she ambled. "A little place called the Wild West out in Dim Q on a planet called Gaia in a town called El Paso out Texas way. Now those were the days."

"See, Drake? You're gonna feel right at home here."

Pete ordered root beer floats for himself and Kyrian who subsequently ordered a round for the house. The tall ice cream glasses reminded Pete of the milkshakes his mother made for him in times of crisis, and for the first time since his arrival, he felt homesick to the verge of tears.

"You okay, bugalugs?" Kyrian asked.

Pete nodded, worried his voice would crack if he spoke.

"Back-to-school blues? Everyone gets 'em. Nothing to be ashamed of."

"But you don't have them," Pete said, looking into Kyrian's contented face.

"Who says?" Kyrian winked at Pete and grabbed some candied baked beans from a bowl on a side table before making one last visit to the Galley bar, leaving Pete alone with his thoughts. "Here, this should help," he said, returning to hand Pete a caramel apple. "You Q-zers have the weirdest food. I can't get enough of it!"

"Ahem," a subdued voice said. Otto hovered nearby, his pocket chronometer dangling at his side.

"Looks like it's that time," Pete said wistfully.

The podmates headed to their room where a new sleep-tunic awaited Pete, hanging on the inside of his closet. He smiled, reflecting on his nights alone in his Appraisement room with no one to keep him company but a speechless orb and Esperança's disembodied voice. This would be the first time he slept with a roommate since he and his brother were little. He had mixed feelings about it. He had mixed feelings about all of it.

After Pete changed into his tunic, Otto floated over to him, toothpaste and brush in each metal-clamp hand.

"Just like home," Pete remarked.

"I beg your pardon, syr?"

"My dad's obsessed with toothbrushing."

"I am certain it is with your best interests in mind, syr."

Pete slouched with guilt for betraying his father's trust by leaving home, but like his father, he'd had the family's *best interests in mind* when he'd done so.

"Posture, Maistr Drake!" Otto enjoined, closing himself inside the armoire for the night.

Pete crawled up into his hammock and stared at the Squallix net on the ceiling. Despite how weary he was, he felt too apprehensive to sleep. He thought about his mother and wondered how she felt her first night in her podroom. If she'd been admitted as a first-level, she would have only been ten or eleven when she lay down in her new bed all those years ago.

Pete tried to picture what her room would have looked like. Located in the Ignis estate, how cozy could it have been?

Not very.

He hoped she'd had a Warden as friendly and helpful as Kyrian to acclimate her. Most of all, he hoped she'd been happy.

{Kapta Fuinenn-Etts}

Chapter Thirty-Six – Up and at 'Em

"Felilum, Fiddleheads!" a perky girl's voice boomed. **"Time to rise and bloom."**

Pete screamed at being startled awake.

"Bennmush to the start of another Ocademy term. It seems like just anthshefflum we were bidding one another <u>bendiarh</u> and parting ways for the twixt-term hiatus. What did you do over the interval, Bilge?"

"Oh, the usual, you know – helped my dads scrape the bone marrow suckers off the house. By the time school gets out, the place is crawling with 'em."

Pete squinted at the image of a pair of irritatingly chipper students at a news desk in a hologram broadcast just feet away from his hammock. Kyrian put his head under his pillow and groaned.

"We here at station AOAS are proud to bring you all the newest news you need to get through these first hectic luum back on campus. Aren't we, Jemm?"

"That's right, Bilge! And for those of you starting your lum with a centering session of Ta'o Qheng, best get a move on. The aurora's almost up!"

Pete rubbed his eyes, fearing he was teetering on a headache. "I don't understand a single thing they're saying."

"Good, then go back to sleep," Kyrian moaned.

Pete was just lying down again when Otto floated out of the armoire carrying Pete's official school uniform.

"Whoaaaaa," Pete whispered.

"Whoa, indeed, syr."

Pete climbed down from his hammock and took the clothing hanger from the Domesticrat's hand, marveling at the ocean-blue embroidered fabric.

"You don't want to be late, Maistr Peyton. And you need your Spoils today of all days."

"What exactly *are* Spoils, Otto?"

"I believe your people refer to it as breaking the fast – most unusual nomenclature."

"Do I put my uniform on before or after I eat?"

"An excellent question, syr. Owing to the newness of both the situation and your finery, I would advise you take your meal first."

Pete stood inert.

"As in *now*, syr."

"Where do I ..."

"The Galley, syr."

"Right." Pete hung his uniform and walked out to the Galley, still wearing his sleep tunic so as not to risk soiling his uniform.

A gaggle of titters came from those in the room at the sight of Pete in his nightwear.

"Oh shush," Cookie said. "If you were smart, you'd do the same ... Now, what can I get you, hon?"

"Uh, do you have French toast?" Pete asked.

"No toast from France, I'm afraid."

"Oh, it's not exactly toast and … Scratch that. How about an English muffin?"

"I have a banana-walnut muffin. But it's from here, not England."

For the sake of time and sanity, Pete nodded.

"Anything to drink?" Cookie asked.

"Do you have orange juice? Orange as in from the fruit, not the county?" Pete joked.

She blinked twice at him. "How about I pour you a cup of tea."

"Yes!" Pete enthused. It felt like ages since he'd first experienced the salubrious effect of a simple cup of tea, and it sounded like just the thing to calm his first-day-of-school nerves.

After adding sugar and milk, he sipped the steaming brew tentatively, not wanting to burn his tongue. Heaven forbid he be unable to speak correctly his first day. The liquid happiness streamed down his throat, warming his soul. It was just as good as he remembered.

Halfway through the muffin he excused himself from the Galley bar, overwrought with worry that he would be late.

Kyrian's probably already dressed and heading out the door.

He dashed back into the podroom and found Kyrian still prone with his head under the pillow.

"I'm gonna throttle those clowns," Kyrian howled.

"What clowns?"

Kyrian pointed toward the bathroom. "And they were worried about *us* being the loud ones? They've been in there yelling over the roar of the shower for the last ten omaa … Worse yet, they're yelling about mathematical equations. Aethereans, take me away!"

Pete cracked the bathroom door open. "Hi guys. Could you maybe keep it down a little. Kyrian is … uh … meditating."

"That fellow meditates?" Benn asked.

"Meditates! About what?" Glenn said.

"He's actually very pious," Pete replied.

Kyrian drowned a fit of laughter in his pillow.

As Otto hovered over to Pete with toothpaste and brush at the ready, Pete made a point to push the bathroom door fully open. Glenn and Benn peered through the doorway to regard Kyrian who was now sitting on the floor in a lotus prayer pose.

🦅🦅🦅

Pete couldn't stop staring at himself in his closet mirror. Getting measured for his uniform had been like trying on a costume for a fancy dress party. But now, wearing it as part of his everyday routine made him feel like someone of importance.

"Like a royal emissary," he whispered aloud.

"You got a bag for your books?" Kyrian asked, buckling his kilt.

Pete shook his head, dazed by how unprepared for class he was.

Kyrian strapped on his sporran and grinned. "Looks like you do now."

Otto labored to stay aloft while holding the handle of an overstuffed leather satchel from which hung a fishnet containing the globe-shaped cyclopedia.

"Oh wow!"

"Too much wow, if you ask me." Kyrian grabbed the bookbag. "Let's see your class skej?"

Pete reached into his pocket and produced the paper that was to be his lifeline for the rest of the day.

"First off you have History and Cosmology ... with ..." Kyrian smiled. "You're in luck. General Alberts is as lax as they come. You won't need this ... and definitely not this," he said, removing the pesky troglodyte tome and netted cyclopedia. "Keep the Ethics book." He stopped to sigh, clutching the paper to his chest and looking dreamily off in the distance.

Pete lifted an eyebrow in puzzlement. "Everything okay, Kyrian?"

Kyrian snapped out of his woolgathering and returned to Pete's class schedule. "... I wouldn't bother with Dimensional Distinctions ... Don't worry about Widgetry. MacIvers always forgets what books he assigns ... And that should do it! Not so bad after all, eh?"

Pete nodded in relief, lifting the bag with moderate ease. "What about *your* books?"

"Never touch the stuff. So, ready for your brain to explode?"

"Only if you mean that figuratively."

"Guess you'll find out." Kyrian gave Pete a friendly slap on the back and strode from the room looking more like a fairy tale hero than a student.

"Thanks, Otto!" Pete called back as he shambled toward the exit, trying to find a comfortable way to schlep the satchel.

He gingerly made his way down the corkscrew staircase taking extra care not to trip and doing his best to keep up with Kyrian. When they arrived at the escalator, Nadalien was already heading to The Wheel—every one of her mechanical steps occupied by a student.

"...Mentis Imperium ... Pachinko ... Paranormal Merry-Making ... Pyromancy," the conveyant drawled.

"Felilum, Nadalien," Kyrian said.

"Felilum to you too, Kyrian. Looking sharp in your new seventh-level kit ... Somatic Defence ... Spavel ... Transmogrification ..."

"Well, this is it, bugalugs," Kyrian said as they disembarked. "Sea ya for Splitz in the Gnook."

"For whats where ... when?" Pete called out as Kyrian disappeared into the crowd.

Pete realized he'd become turned around and couldn't make out which way was which. Nothing looked familiar. He peered down at his class schedule, but people kept bumping him, and he couldn't focus on the printed words. Trying in vain to steady the page, his gaze drifted to the colorful pie-shaped wedges painted on the floor—color codes he'd been unable to see when viewing the jammed Wheel from Kyrian's shoulders.

He followed the blue wedge as it fanned out, successfully making his way to the Blueberry sector. There, each of the classrooms was designated with a sign on its door. All were written in English.

"Thank the Aethereans!" he said under his breath.

Within seconds, he located his class:

History & Cosmology

General Alberts

Classroom ~ Open

Observatory ~ Not Today

He put a clammy hand on the doorknob, seriously considering returning to the Pod, then turned the knob and entered. The seated students stared at him.

What, is there something coming out of my nose?

He took the nearest vacant seat and furtively wiped his nostrils.

A hush fell over the room as a raggedy man with wild grey hair and a matching mustache tootled in wearing a worn-out cardigan and house slippers, his hands in his trouser pockets. "History – bah! Who vants to read droning accounts of dead people ve have never met und who have no connection to us vhatsoever? ... Do you? ... Vhat about you?"

All eyes followed him as he doddered around the classroom.

"So tell me, vat do these stories about people in overgrown graves from dimensions that have long since vanished have to do vith you? Eh? ... I vill tell you. They are your roadmaps for life. From them you can learn, *must* learn, how thoughts can lead to vords and vords to deeds. That actions have conseqvences und those conseqvences have conseqvences of their own. And so I ask you ... vhat vill be your history? ... Please take out your writing implements."

As the students burrowed into their knapsacks and pockets, Pete momentarily panicked, knowing he had none of his usual writing equipment from home. He cursed his father. He cursed pen-purloiner Sally Daniels. He cursed himself for not being better prepared. Hoping for a miracle, he reached into his bookbag and was overjoyed to find a stack of dried seaweed sheets. Slipped under their raffia tie was a kelp bulb with a shaft that tapered down to a fine point. He gave the shoot a gentle squeeze, and a drop of squid ink bubbled out.

Otto to the rescue again.

"I have an assignment for you all … Are you ready?"

The students sat poised over their desks like runners at their starting blocks.

"Your assignment is to write down how you vant to be remembered. Vhat you vant your history to be – your legacy. After you are finished, I vant you to lock avay your answer until the end of the term. Give it to your Domesticrat for safe-keeping if you must, but don't look at it until I tell you. Is that understood?"

All nodded.

"Sehr gut. That is all for today. Now go make some history."

Make history? I'm not even sure how to make my new bed!

{Kapta Fuinenn-Rreh}

CHAPTER THIRTY-SEVEN — "PROMISE NOT TO KILL ME."

A cloud of questions swirled through Pete's mind as he exited the classroom. Where was his next class, what would his legacy be, and why did his teacher look like Albert Einstein? First things first—he should take advantage of the abbreviated class period and the lack of people in the Wheel by locating the rest of his classes.

"How're things going?" a familiar voice called in his head.

"Esperança?" he whispered.

"In the flesh ... Well, maybe not exactly," she giggled.

"What are you doing here?"

"Just came to check on you. How're you managing in Aquis so far? I know it wasn't your first pick."

"It's amazing, actually. My podmate is this guy named Kyrian. I don't remember his last name, but anyway, he's really cool. And so's his accent, kinda like Australian but not really. Anyway, do you know who he is?"

"Everyone at the Ocademy knows who he is. Most would like to know him better, to put it politely."

"Yeah, he's hard to miss. He's a good guy too. He's really been helping me learn the ins and outs of the place."

"That's wonderful news! And you know, it's an awfully big compliment that Aquis pushed so hard for you. Legacies are rarely allowed to be adopted out. It was expected you'd go to Ignis."

"Maybe Ignis didn't want me."

"Oh they wanted you, all right. The offspring of Cassiopeia Salvatori? You're like Byzantine gold to them."

"So then why'd they let me go?"

"I've been wondering about that myself. Whichever one of us finds out first tells the other. Pact?"

"If that means *do we have a deal*, yes, pact!"

"I better get going. I have a report to give on the effect of gamma rays on man-in-the-moon marigolds. Nice catching up with you, Pete."

"You too, Espa."

Between General Alberts' rousing speech and Esperança's comments about Aquis and Ignis vying for him, Pete felt on top of the world—like he had worth and true purpose. It didn't matter that he didn't know what that purpose was. Just having one was good enough at the moment. Wearing a snazzy new uniform didn't hurt either.

He made short work of finding the rest of his classes, then waited outside the Ethics classroom for the period in session to dismiss. After observing several students weeping as they exited, he decided to sit in the back of the class.

Preceptor Elora Windwalker glided into the room without a sound. She was tall and lithe with dark green eyes and flowing aubergine hair pulled off her face in a Celtic knot. Pete clutched the edge of his desk when he caught a glimpse of her pointy ears.

She's an elf!

Her demeanor was at once warm but reserved, and she made him nervous. Though he didn't follow a thing she said, he couldn't take his eyes off her. He was glad Kyrian suggested toting the Ethics textbook, as the pupils were asked to refer to it several times. At least he thought they were—he couldn't be sure. He was too entranced by Elora to recall what happened exactly.

He greeted his next class, Somatic Defence (known in his home realm as Martial Arts), with far less enchantment.

Great. Athletics. The lethal kind, no less.

After all were seated on the kwoon's floor mats, a small man concealed up in the corner of the ceiling dropped down silently into the middle of the room. Doyen Mai T. Mite's stature came up to around Pete's chest, and he looked to weigh about as much as the pumpkin Pete's family carved for All Hallows Eve the year prior. Even so, the diminutive figure was someone Pete would not wish to cross in a dark alley.

When a pupil asked if the class would involve the use of weapons, Doyen Mite said, "Yes. And *you* are that weapon."

The class was basic, geared to first- through fifth-levels with groups sectioned off according to experience. Within the first ten minutes, the patient but firm Preceptor had the Fiddleheads using proper form and practicing stances. Pete was happily surprised to find he understood the concepts and managed to get through the moves without looking too ridiculous.

The following class, Dimensional Distinctions, was agony for Pete. In the core course comprised of first- and second-levels, the teacher treated everyone like they were children, which most of them were. Preceptor Feffer started the session by asking the pupils to take out their textbooks with the goal of helping the fledgling Fiddleheads with *the big words.*

They never got beyond the book's cover.

Now I know why Kyrian said not to bother bringing my book.

It didn't take long for Pete to start thinking like an Ocademy skolier. Without assistance from Esperança or Kyrian, he figured out the *Zenith* noted on his schedule referred to *noon, Splitz* was the term for *lunch*, and the Comestibles Commons most likely referred to the sphinx-guarded dining hall off The Hub. At least he hoped so, because that's where he was going, presumably to meet Kyrian.

When he arrived at the entrance, he watched in amazement as students blithely rambled past the sphinx.

If Demetrius can stand up to the rebels, I can get past the sphinx.

Steeling himself, he gulped and gave a low bow. "Nice to see you, Sahrlaah."

She bowed her head in response. Pete scampered by, avoiding eye contact.

Entering the noisy room, he espied several tables occupied by students in ocean-blue liveries. A cluster of girls all giggling demurely and looking at a specific table in the sea of blue suggested the spot where Kyrian was sitting. As Pete made his way to the table, the hairs on his arms raised under the watch of a giant, bronze, winged robot that circled overhead.

Why do I suddenly feel like prey?

He took the empty seat next to Kyrian, keeping an eye on the ceiling.

"Wondering what's going on with Talos, eh?" Kyrian asked.

"Is that his name? If so, yeah. He's making me kinda uncomfortable."

"He's actually here to protect you."

"Me?"

"You and the rest of us. The Bureau hired him right after that Caretaker holovid was hijacked by XQ. Make sure not to do anything suspicious. If Talos thinks you have malevolent intentions, he'll bathe himself in fire and enfold you in his searing grasp. That's gotta be the worst way to cark it." Kyrian shuddered.

"Can I get my food to go?" Pete said, trying not to make any sudden moves that could attract the attention of the flying metal colossus.

Kyrian mussed Pete's hair. "You'll be fine. Tell me, how did class go?"

"A lot better than I would've thought, except for one thing that's driving me crazy."

Kyrian's eyes widened with interest. "About Ethics class?"

"History and Cosmology actually. The Preceptor who teaches it. He totally reminds me of someone who was famous on my planet. But he died like nearly a hundred years ago."

"You mean Albert Einstein?"

Pete's mouth fell open. "How did you know?"

Kyrian guffawed. "I know cuz everyone in the Omniverse knows. He's known across the dimensions!"

"Don't you think General Alberts looks just like him?"

Kyrian blinked at him blankly. "Just when I thought you were so smart. He *is* Albert Einstein!"

"What? But how?"

"You're taking his Spavel class, right?"

Pete nodded.

"*That's* how."

Pete still wasn't sold. "Okay, if that's him, why does everyone call him General Alberts?"

"He tried to go incognito when he first arrived. Supposedly he was hiding from some mad dictator from your realm who wanted him to build bombs or something. Anyway, when he got here, he introduced himself as Dr. Alberts, but it was obvious to everyone who he was. He got the nickname General from the abbreviation Gen Rel – as in General Relativity, his renowned science theory."

"Ohhhhhhhh pretty clever. What *is* General Relativity, by the way?"

"Your guess is as good as mine. I've heard the answer anenn times and still can't explain it." Kyrian tapped on the table to get Pete back on track. "What about the rest of your Preceptors?"

"Dimensional Distinctions was the worst! Preceptor Feffer talked to us like we were babies."

"When it comes to knowledge of the Omniverse, you *are* a baby, bugalugs ... Soooo ... what did you think of ... your Ethics Preceptor?"

Pete looked both ways before whispering his answer. "She's an elf!"

Kyrian let out an enamored sigh. "Yes, she is! She just started teaching last sekkl and thrash it, I'd already filled my Ethics quota. I'm considering doing something unethical so they'll make me take the class again."

Pete exchanged smiles with a girl who walked by. "Hey, Kevlin."

"New friend?" Kyrian asked.

"We kinda met during Appraisement and she was my partner in Somatic Defence today. It sure was different than I expected."

"Oh?"

"Yeah, it was so ... I don't know ... peaceful. I thought Doyen Mite would be all angry and go around shouting and kicking things, but he was really calm. And he had an assistant who helped make sure everyone stood up straight and had their arms and legs turned the right way. She was really subdued, like Doyen Mite."

"Black hair on one side, silver on the other, with a black circle on the silver side and vice versa?"

"Yes! I recognized her from the Melt-a-Malefactor booth at the Ignis carnival during Appraisement. Do you know her?"

"Better than I'd care to. That's Yinyang. Be careful around her. You never know which side of her you're dealing with. She's a firecracker – heck of a fighter too. I should know." Kyrian lifted his shirt to reveal a large bruise on his ribs. "As you can see, seventh-level Somatic Defence isn't so *subdued* ... Ah, here comes our food now. Ceviche! Bonzers! Still wiggling and everything!"

They continued chitchatting about their classes as they supped, the hope of an Edni sighting always in the back of Pete's mind.

"Hey, Demo's here. I need to go talk to him about something he's planning," Kyrian garbled as he spooned the last vestiges of seafood into his mouth. "You okay on your own?"

Pete nodded, immediately scanning the room in search of Edni. Failing to locate her, he cleared his place and exited the dining hall. On the landing, he found the sphinx in a state of agitation, her back paw whacking away at her ear.

His fear at being clawed by her was trumped only by his empathy for her plight of having an itch she didn't seem able to scratch. "I think I can help," he called out to her in a loud whisper. "But you have to promise not to kill me."

She retracted her claws and laid her head down.

As he climbed up on the mammoth beast's front shoulder, she curled her paws beneath her torso and grimaced. Pete roughly scratched behind her ear. She tipped her head toward him, and he scratched more vigorously. After a three-inch Mydas fly flew out of the sphinx's ear, Pete ceased scratching. "I think we got it," he panted. "I sure hope you feel better."

She let out a long moan, then licked her lips and rested her head on her front paws.

Pete dismounted with a feeling of accomplishment sprinkled with daring. The feeling surprised him. He was unaccustomed to attempting anything beyond his basic level of comfort. He generally strove to coast through life without making ripples, definitely without conflict, and preferably without change.

Even so, he liked the changes he was beginning to see in himself since coming to the academy—changes that hinted at the heroic character of his mother. He hoped his father would notice the changes too and be proud of him.

Mom ... Dad ... parents ... family. Dang it! I still haven't called home!

With time to spare before his next class, he decided to pay a visit to The Soup Can communications store. Walking past the queues outside the shops along the way, he was thrilled to find The Soup Can free of long lines and crowds.

"Hi. Do you have any devices that can contact Dimension Q?" he asked as he strolled into the empty, tired-looking shop.

"I do," said a haggard clerk as he chewed on the end of an unlit cigarillo.

"May I have one, please?"

The clerk shifted the cigarillo to the other side of his mouth and sat back on his barstool. "No, you may not."

"I'm a fourth-level, not a first, if that makes any difference."

"I knew you were a fourth-level the minute I set eyes on you," the clerk said, waving his cigarillo at Pete's uniform.

"Oh … well … then why can't I get a Dimension Q contactor thing?"

"Bureau rules, too risky at present – rebellion and all. There goes my livelihood, all for the sake of student safety. Backward priorities if you ask me."

Unsure how to respond, Pete forced a smile and simply walked out the door.

He continued around the perimeter of The Hub, looking for one of the multidirectional escalators to take him down to the Wheel. When he came to an unoccupied dilapidated conveyant, he stopped at its landing, trying to determine if the escalator was operational.

"Class level?" asked a gruff voice like that of a wizened New York cabbie that smoked too much.

"Oh! You work."

"Of course, I work! I'm no freeloader. Ya think I'm lazy or somethin'? Why, I oughta—"

"Sorry, I, uh, yes, the class level would be great … please."

"Well climb on then. I don't got all day, ya know."

Pete stepped on, and the rickety moving stairway chugged its way down one floor.

"Thanks, sir," Pete said, stepping off into the Wheel area.

"Don't mention it," the conveyant wheezed.

Pete had no trouble following the red floor wedge to the Cherry sector where his next class, M.A.G.I.C., was located, but as he approached the door, he realized he hadn't brought any of the items needed for his afternoon courses.

Maybe if I ran back to the dining hall, I could at least collect the carrots for M.A.G.I.C., but then I'd risk being late. Dang it!

He entered the M.A.G.I.C. laboratory and frowned at the sight of his podmate Benn sitting alone wearing the full tuxedo ensemble described on the materials list, Benn's gloved hands folded on top of his desk, his too small top hat precariously perched atop his strawberry-shaped head.

"Who are you?" a large man bellowed at Pete, storming in from a backroom and tripping over the hem of a deep-purple tunic decorated with small swirling galaxies and shooting stars that whizzed across the fabric. His matching pointy cap flopped over one eye, defying him each time he tried to move it to the side of his head.

Pete couldn't decide if the man was dressed as a wizard or dressed for bed. "I'm Pete Drake, sir."

"Of course you are. Who else would you be?" He tucked up his long robe and strode from the room, then returned with a hanger attached to what looked like a small bedroll. "Here, this came for you. Better use my office in case … Well, just in case."

Pete accepted the parcel tentatively and inched toward the office, hoping not to find out what *just in case* might involve.

It's times like this I wish I had a hazmat suit.

{Kapta Fuinenn-Ipi}

Chapter Thirty-Eight – Codswallop

Pete stepped into Preceptor MacIvers office, uncertain exactly what he was expected to do while there. Holding his breath, he cautiously unlashed the buckle on the roll, and a leather garment bag unfurled. After a moment of indecision, he unsnapped the bag and discovered his tuxedo and other materials needed for class.

Thanks, Otto. You're a lifesaver.

It took him some doing to figure out how to put everything on, and he got things wrong more than once. Fortunately, his black bow tie was pre-tied and simply needed to be fastened in the back. After donning his top hat and gloves, he looked around the cluttered room for a full-length mirror, hoping to catch a glimpse of his outfit—he'd never worn a tuxedo before.

As he swaggered out of the office to take a seat, he stopped to deposit some of the requisite carrots on the Preceptor's desk.

"In my day, pupils gave their teachers apples," Preceptor MacIvers commented with a genial grin.

A pair of young students entered, both wearing their first-level uniforms. Pete felt a twinge of sympathy for them as clearly, they too had forgotten to bring their formalwear. When the class filled, Pete realized only he and Benn were wearing tuxedos. Abashed, he stealthily removed his top hat and placed his gloves and bow tie inside it, hiding it under his seat. He then slid out of his tux jacket, trying to look as inconspicuous as possible. Benn, on the other hand, held his top-hatted head high.

"Who can tell me what magic is?" Preceptor MacIvers asked, the resonance of his voice like that of someone who just swallowed a spoonful of peanut butter.

Benn raised his gloved hand.

"Who are you, little man?"

"Benn Snodgrass, Dim Delta, first-level Aquis."

"Tell me what you know about magic, Benn Snodgrass."

"Magic: the supernatural power to influence events and translate matter using various spells, substances, and activating tools such as wands and charms."

"Very detailed description, Snodgrass."

Benn laced his gloved fingers. "I concur, Preceptor MacIvers."

"And absolute rubbish!"

The class broke out in sniggers.

"M.A.G.I.C. ... Mental acuity gelds insidious codswallop, my friends," the Preceptor said, sweeping his hand in front of him as he spoke. "Mindlessness and guesswork induce codswallop ... Meretricious abracadabra gesturing is codswallop! Anyone see a pattern here? ... No one? ... What about you in the back hiding his tuxedo."

Pete flinched at the tuxedo mention. "Umm, codswallop?"

"Exactly! That's what the idea most people believe about magic is – codswallop, mumbo jumbo, claptrap, malarkey, flummery, poppycock!" He pounded his fist on his desk in punctuation, causing those in the front row to jolt in their seats. "You want to move things without your hands? You don't need a wand for that. You only need a passing grade in Mentis Imperium, Preceptor Seeford's mental arts class."

Some of the students chuckled, others simply dangled their jaws.

"You want charms? Lyria Corden's Manipulation and Espionage class will teach you how to charm your way in or out of any situation, no talismans required."

Benn raised his hand. "I believe the Manipulation and Espionage course was cancelled."

"Oh you're right."

"I know I am," Benn replied, his top hat sliding off the back of his head as he lifted his chin in unabashed egotism.

"You can thank the rebels for that – killjoys! … What was I talking about?"

"Codswallop?" said a tiny young girl carrying a doll that looked just like her.

"Yes! Codswallop! Now, who among you is dying to learn how to initiate the metamorphosis of substances?"

As hands raised, he motioned for the students to come closer.

Chairs squeaked in sync as rapt listeners leaned forward.

MacIvers shielded his mouth with his hand and whispered. "Crack open a pair of cackleberries, squeeze in the secretions of a bovine, mix those together with some ground wheat, toss in a few roasted cacao nibs and *bake a cake*!"

A few of the students groaned in disappointment. Most just looked confused. Benn took notes—wearing his dress gloves.

"Magic is real, Fiddleheads," the Preceptor boomed. "And it goes on all around us every day. In this class, you will learn where to look for it, how to tap into it, how to get at the truth behind the illusion. We're going to do some demythtifying and plenty of it, have no fear. Now who's with me?!"

No one made a peep. Pete raised his hand.

"Yes? You have a question?"

"No, sir, umm I was raising my hand to show I'm *with* you."

Preceptor MacIvers held his stomach and let out a big rumbling belly laugh. "Good man! What's your name again?"

"Uh, Drake," he mumbled.

"Just Drake? I thought there was more to it than that."

"Pete Drake, actually."

A few heads belonging to students wearing red and black flame-logo uniforms whipped around. Eyes narrowed in disapproval. Furious whispers bubbled up in clusters throughout the classroom.

Pete wanted to bolt from the room, to get away from the world, to crawl out from under his mother's legacy, and especially to be free of people's expectations of him. Unfortunately, he knew running away would only give his scoffers yet another reason to mock him.

"Settle down, everyone," Preceptor MacIvers said.

I wonder how Demetrius or Kyrian would handle this situation. Dumb question. They'd never be in this situation.

Pete picked at his thumbnails while his pancreas squeezed in on itself.

"He's nothing like his mother," Benn snarked, turning to face the class. "I should know. I'm his pinmate."

That kid's really starting to get my goat!

"That's quite enough, Snotgrass," MacIvers warned.

"It's Snodgrass, syr."

"Not anymore."

The corner of Pete's mouth crept into a smile.

Pete stayed after class long enough to change back into his uniform in MacIvers' office while the Preceptor addressed the concerns of an animal activist who was up in arms about the treatment of rabbits in magic shows and the use of their feet as good-luck charms.

As Pete meandered toward his next class, he cogitated on the quality of his education back home.

I wonder if I would've learned more if I'd had teachers like the ones here at the academy?

He already liked three of his Preceptors, and was thrilled to have two classes each with Alberts and MacIvers. Conversely, he couldn't remember the names of his teachers at his last school.

He effortlessly found his way to the Spavel classroom, stopping to read the sign on the door before turning the knob.

Spavel

General Alberts

Classroom: Open

Nexus: Accessible by Preceptor Invitation Only. (Don't hold your breath)

He didn't understand what Spavel was all about, but felt certain General Alberts would make it entertaining. The fact the classroom annexed a space that could be accessed only by invitation from the Preceptor instantly made the class more intriguing.

Pete entered the boisterous room to find bunches of students in heated discussions over their personal theories about the inner workings of time and space travel based on their favorite book series, long-running television shows, and film franchises. The topics of teleportation, sonic gadgets, prophetic visioning, gender-bending, and molecular regeneration spawned the most debate.

He attempted to take a seat several times, only to be told the desk in question was already spoken for. Apparently, Spavel was a popular subject.

General Alberts eventually tottered into class, his trademark cardigan buttoned incorrectly. "Apologies for my tardiness. I lost track of the time. Imagine, losing track of something that does not even exist!" His eyes twinkled as he spoke, his passion for the subject matter contagious. "So ... who here vould give his grandmother to travel through time?"

The majority of hands raised.

"Vhat about traveling through space? … I see only a few hands. Traveling through space is something ve do everyday, ja? So then, is it possible to do both? Before you answer, please be avare I speak in terms of reality, not fantastical fandom."

Easy chuckles floated through the classroom as students communicated with each other using the gestures associated with their favorite fandoms.

The rest of the class was a blur for Pete who knew nothing about the space-time continuum or quarks or redshift or any of the terms General Alberts bandied about as if he were explaining something as simple as how to button a cardigan sweater—bad example.

Although it had been an easy day, Pete was exhausted and worried he'd never get through his next two classes without falling asleep. Even more distressing, he still had to deal with the ballyhooed sport of Squallix. He hadn't the foggiest notion what it involved and didn't particularly care, because he'd made up his mind to find a way *not* to play. Surely, inexperience and ineptitude could be counted on for something.

🦇🦇🦇

When he arrived in the Widgetry workshop, he found Preceptor MacIvers dressed in a Hawaiian shirt and Bermuda shorts, sans footwear. Considering the course materials list included steel-toed boots, Pete cringed to think what might befall the teacher's toes.

"Drake," MacIvers called, waving Pete over. "This came for you."

The burly man hoisted a brown-paper parcel onto his long workbench and walked away humming, carrying a cordless drill and pressing the trigger to the rhythm of a song Pete recognized well. His parents called it *their song*. Prior to Pete's tenth birthday, they used to sing it at the top of their lungs when it came on the car radio. And they danced to it as it played on the living room hi-fi each year on their wedding anniversary.

The thought of his parents pulled him up short.

&^%! *I need to find a way to contact home, one way or another.*

He opened the package and found the Widgetry textbook, the materials for his next class, a ripe Honeycrisp apple, and a note from Otto suggesting Pete consume the apple to keep his energy up.

Pete really liked having a valet.

He tucked the fruit into his pocket and walked by MacIvers' desk where a <u>Newton's cradle</u> lazily swung and clacked. Remembering what MacIvers had said about teachers receiving apples back in *his day*, Pete stopped, took a step backward, removed the apple from his pocket, and placed it on the Preceptor's desk. He then selected a seat in the second row. It was closer to the front than he usually chose to sit, but he liked Preceptor MacIvers, and this was the class that excited him most.

MacIvers picked up the apple, smiling broadly and looking around the room in search of the donor. When he took a loud crunchy bite, Pete felt all was right with the world—that is until Benn showed up wearing industrial safety goggles and heavy-duty work gloves, taking the seat diagonally in front of Pete, partially obscuring his sight lines.

Ah well, Cassiopeia Salvatori Drake's son wasn't about to let a pest like Benn Snodgrass steal his serenity.

"Is this seat taken?" a nasally voice said as Clybe slid into the chair next to Benn directly in front of Pete, effectively eclipsing Pete's view of anything but Clybe's big head.

Pete slumped in his chair, temporarily down, but not out.

{Kapta Fuinenn-Oneu}

CHAPTER THIRTY-NINE – SPUNT THOSE REBELS!

Found Music was Pete's last period of the day, and it took every ounce of energy he had left to drag himself into the office at the Plum sector's junkyard where the class convened that afternoon. He was in no mood to rummage through decaying garbage in search of noisemakers. He just wanted to take a nap and maybe have a cup of tea —or both.

When all the students had squeezed into the dump's teeny office, a curvaceous woman with the voice of a nightingale appeared in the doorway, her hands elegantly posed by her sides.

"Right this way, doves," she said in a singsong tone. "Nose-clamps will not be necessary."

She led the group out to a plush knoll covered in clover and cornflowers, encircled by blossoming trees. As she walked, she stopped here and there to collect twigs that she wove together into a patterned disk. Pete wondered if she was some kind of witch— certainly, her voice had bewitched him.

"Please," she said, gesturing to the students to sit on the ground. "I am your Found Music Preceptor, Lyria Corden. Welcome to one of the most soul-satisfying courses in the Omni curriculum. Sages have long noted that music is the purest and most evocative language in the Omniverse. And legend has it music was what led to the existence of Aquis. When Deora, the grand creatrix, heard the auroral stars singing together for the first time, she was so moved, she shed a tear. That

First Tear as it is known, marked the beginning of water, and is celebrated annually as a cherished <u>Jalilum</u>."

Pete sat a bit taller at the mention of Aquis, *his* element.

"In this class, you will learn to find music in everything and everyone you encounter each and every lum, beginning now. Please, lie back on the grass ... That's right, doves, go ahead and get comfortable ... Now close your eyes and listen. Don't speak, don't think, just listen. And yes, it's all right if you slumber. In fact, it's encouraged."

Pete wasted no time following the teacher's orders.

Best class ever! Best teacher ever!

Birdsong wafted through the air, underpinned by the throaty whisper of breeze through the trees. Soon a chorus of snores added to the symphony.

"Class dismissed," the dulcet voice cooed.

Pete blinked his eyes open, trying to get his bearings, and momentarily questioning if he was at the park back home having dreamt the whole academy experience. When he propped himself up on his elbows, he saw the comely instructor standing and smiling down at her bleary brood who were as reluctant to depart the tranquil knoll as Pete was.

He picked up his hefty bag and staggered back toward the Wheel, not bothering to consider where he was to go next. Intuitively, he found his way to Nadalien where a steady stream of dog-tired Fiddleheads slogged onto the coquettish conveyant's moving steps, heads down and faces drooping.

When at last he made it up the stairs and into the podroom, he was shocked to find Kyrian a bundle of unbridled energy—energy that fatigued Pete just to watch.

"Did you find your days' supplies satisfactory, syr?" Otto asked Pete, catching Pete's satchel as its strap slid off Pete's shoulder.

Pete wanted to tell Otto how much he appreciated all the things the Domesticrat had done for him throughout the day, from the tuxedo to the books to the apple, but all he could muster to say was, "Thanks."

Kyrian zipped up a duffle bag the size of Pete's not-so little brother then turned his enthusiasm toward Pete. "Shake a leg, bugalugs. It's time for the greatest experience of your young Fiddlehead life. It's time for Squallix!"

Pete collapsed into his desk chair. He'd already determined he'd have to pretend to be sick to get out of going to Squallix—no two ways about it. He felt his forehead, hoping it was warm from all the book carting so he could claim a fever.

Kyrian rolled his shoulders and stretched his neck side to side in preparation. "And don't even think about trying to get out of it!"

Demetrius blew into the room, his cheeks flushed. Pete knew he stood no chance of saying no to the two godlike sportsmen standing before him. That thought alone made him feverish.

"Did you hear?" Demetrius asked Kyrian.

"Hear what?"

"No Squallix today."

"What?!" Kyrian roared, his voice ringing through the Frond.

Demetrius shook his head. "Damage from the tsunami. Spunt those rebels!"

Pete nodded in solidarity, doing his best not to smile at the news of the cancellation.

"For how long?!" Kyrian demanded.

"No telling. All I know is they won't let any of us near the field today."

Kyrian dropped into his desk chair, a broken man.

Demetrius put a hand on his shoulder. "I know … If you want, we can go over some new plays I've been working on."

"No … thanks, Demo. I'm good. I kinda just want to … I dunno."

Pete's relief was matched only by his sympathy for Kyrian. For whatever reason, Squallix was Kyrian's greatest joy, and Pete was saddened to see his good-natured podmate so crestfallen. Pete knew all too well the feeling of looking forward to something for ages, only to have all hope dashed at the last minute. It had happened to Pete occasionally throughout the last five years. Nearly always it was his father's doing, accompanied by some speech about how Pete should buck up and get over it.

"All that fuss over a doltish frolic. So infantile," Glenn said to Benn, passing by the open door and commenting on Kyrian's reaction to the Squallix situation. "It's not as though he lost a loved one in a rebel attack."

"Or lost his wallet," Benn replied.

"Or received a failing grade."

"Well, we can't be sure of that."

Glenn and Benn both snickered, entering their podroom.

Pete's jaw dropped upon hearing their callous comments about Kyrian.

"And there's no word on when the field will open again?" Kyrian asked, paying no attention to Glenn and Benn's prattle.

Demetrius shook his head and took a seat on the top of Kyrian's box stairs. "None ... None good, anyway. The arena's chief engineer says if the damage is bad enough they'll have to shut the Squallix field down for the whole term. The only thing that's certain is that for now, we're landlocked."

Kyrian froze and just stared ahead not blinking—and Pete feared, not breathing.

Glenn and Benn made their way into the shared bathroom where they continued their mocking discourse.

"Well, when one lacks the cerebral capacities for anything other than childish games ..." Benn remarked coolly.

Glenn replied, "True, one must work within the parameters of one's abilities, limited though they may be."

Pete seethed at the slights.

Benn sighed. "Oh for the simplicity of being simple."

"Agreed," Glenn replied wistfully.

Pete's oft-clenched pancreas sent a surge of pent-up angst flowing out to his fists. They were doing the clenching now, and Pete didn't know how long he could keep them from taking action.

"You know what they say about fellows with large muscles ..." Benn said.

"They are compensating for small brains!" Glenn said.

Those weaselly little twerps are nothing but snobby bullies! How dare they make fun of someone as nice as Kyrian. It's not right!

Glenn and Benn laughed merrily.

I don't care if there's two of them and only one of me. I've had it with bullies!

Glenn shouted over the water running in the bathroom sink. "I suspect the disappointment from a potential full-term arena closure will require the lout to seek out counseling."

"Clearly anyone that wrapped up in sporting activities should get counseling anyway."

They laughed even more heartily.

Without warning, something in Pete snapped. It was one thing for Benn to make wisecracks about Pete not living up to his mother's reputation. But picking on kindhearted Kyrian was going too far. After years of cowering from smug bullies at school and home, Pete had had enough.

"There's nothing childish about it!" Pete shouted, springing out of his chair and hastening to the open bathroom doorway. "Squallix is one of the most challenging and strategic sports ever invented. It's the form of athletics preferred by kings and scholars. And it's no secret Squallix plays and maneuvers have been studied and used as the basis for some of the most successful military campaigns in history. Of course you'd know that if you were half as knowledgeable about the sport as Kyrian. Just today I heard someone in The Hub say the tactics of Squallix may very well be the key Omni needs to defeat the rebels!"

He had no idea where his diatribe came from and even less idea what any of it meant. All he knew was that the two imperious slugs next door had crossed a line in poking fun at Kyrian, and Pete had no intention of letting the affront go unanswered. If lambasting the pair of intellectual elitists had repercussions or meant ostracism by those in the Frond, so be it. It was a matter of integrity—and friendship.

Glenn, Benn, Kyrian, and Demetrius all looked at Pete slack-jawed. When Kyrian and Demetrius approached Pete, Glenn and Benn scurried back to their room like rats chased away from a dumpster. Kyrian and Demetrius pulled Pete out into the hallway and lifted him up onto their shoulders, parading him into the Familial Forum, chanting, "Drake, Drake, Drake, Drake."

Several podroom doors opened in response.

Even Cookie came out of the Galley to see what the ruckus was about. "Why do I get the feelin' I'm gonna be wheedled to whip up something special?"

"Because special occasions call for something just as special. And nothing's more special than Cookie's cooking," Demetrius said, charming the Galleymaster.

Cookie shook her head, all smiles as she unlocked and opened the snack bar.

The podroom doors of the curious closed.

"Anything you want, it's on me!" Kyrian told Pete.

"I wouldn't mind a double chocolate cookie milkshake, if it's not too much trouble," Pete said, bouncing on the trapeziuses of the two hulks beneath him.

"Is it too much trouble, Cookie?" Kyrian called out.

"Anything for you and Demetrius. You know that," she said, pulling a variety of ingredients from her secret stash beneath the Galley bar.

"You mean anything for my podmate, Peyt, here!"

Nobody had ever called him Peyt before. He liked the way it sounded.

As Cookie's blender whirred into life, Demetrius and Kyrian tossed Pete off their shoulders and onto a watercouch. He bobbed as the liquid in the sofa redistributed, his expression locked in an exultant grin.

"They were right about you, Drake," Demetrius said, beaming at Pete.

Pete didn't know who *they* were or what they were right about, but at that moment, he didn't care. He'd scored one for the underdog—an underdog who by all accounts was one of the most popular students on campus, but in the current situation, an underdog nonetheless.

Cookie delivered an overflowing old-fashioned fountain glass to Pete, garnished with a chocolate wafer. "One double chocolate cookie milkshake, on the house!"

"Splendiferest Galleymaster in the Omniverse," Kyrian said, giving Cookie a smooch on the cheek that she waved away with a giggle and a swish of her dish towel.

Pete chugged the shake down straight, feeling too virile to bother with a straw. Not even the threat of brain freeze from the ice cream could daunt him at that triumphant moment.

Kyrian plopped on the couch beside him, causing them both to bob. "Where did you learn all that stuff? That's kwarps beyond Sheffield."

"Actually … I made it up."

Kyrian and Demetrius shared a stupefied look before bursting into laughter, at turns choking in hilarity.

"Now you know why I fought so hard to snatch him from Ignis," Demetrius wheezed. "He's worth every talent we spent."

Kyrian nodded and coughed, raising a thumb in approval.

"You invite him to our meetings yet?" Demetrius asked.

Kyrian shook his head, still choking.

Pete suspected the meetings in question were study sessions. He'd never much enjoyed group study sessions. But not even the thought of that unpleasant activity could pull him down from his current high—even if Glenn and Benn were part of the study group.

"You have to stand up to oppressors, right, Drake?" Demetrius said. "Agitators who try to disrupt the peace and sow seeds of dissension must be routed out. Can I count on you to join us?"

Unclear as to what study sessions had to do with bullies, Pete simply gurgled.

"I'm hungry too," Kyrian said in response. "Wanna head on over to the Gnook? It's nearly Gloaming."

"The nook?" Pete asked.

Kyrian stood and held out his hand to help Pete up. "That's what we call the dining hall. Comestibles Commons is just too much of a mouthful."

"Good idea," Demetrius said, striding toward the exit. "And since we're early, there's somewhere I wanna stop first."

Pete followed, somewhat bemused and not particularly hungry after the milkshake. When they got to the corkscrew stairway, there was no choice to be made. This was a time to take the winding slide and do so with abandon!

"So how did it feel, Drake?" Demetrius asked as Pete steadied himself at the bottom of the slide.

"The slide? It was really fun!"

Demetrius chuckled. "Noooo. I mean how did it feel to take a stand like you did with your sanctimonious pinmates?"

"Oh, I, uh, pretty good I guess."

"That's the sort of gumption that will see us through what's to come. I'm relying on you to help us when we face our greatest foe."

"Well, I've never actually played Squallix before, so I don't know how much help I'd be."

Demetrius and Kyrian both laughed warmly.

"No, Drake." Demetrius put an arm around Pete's shoulder and ushered him through the underwater tunnel as several large sea creatures on the other side of the glass kept pace with them. "I don't mean when we face a Squallix rival. I mean when we take on the rebels. Be prepared to up your game. You're swimming with the big fish now."

THE END

of Pete playing small

HOPEFULLY HELPFUL GLOSSARY
of terms that may be foreign to you depending on your species and dimension of origin

LEGEND:
* *Naturim language word(s) spelled phonetically in the modern People's Parlance*
" *Quoted phrase*
^ *Reference regarding the sport of Squallix*

Adopt out – An academy accommodation whereby a legacy recruit is allowed to leave their element and be inducted by another.

Anthshefflum – The word for *yesterday* in Naturim.

Aquin – A member of the Aquis domain.

Archipelagian League^ – A bustling confederation of competing vocational Squallix squads.

Awiding – What in Dimension Q is known as *going abroad*; the experience whereby a student goes to a foreign land for one school term or an entire school year.

Beamer – A member of the Song of the Sun zell (zealous cult-like organization). Beamers are known for their beaming smiles and sunny dispositions.

Beluga Quartet – This four-whale singing group is a venerated tradition at the Ocademy, with auditions held only once every three seekkl in keeping with species reproductive cycles. Both male and female belugas are welcome to try out for the Sea Canary Choir as the quartet is lovingly nicknamed.

Bendiarh – The word for *farewell, goodbye* in Naturim.

Bilmin – Slang for *very, totally, utterly.*

Bone marrow suckers – Attaching to sentients and architectural structures alike, these chatty vermin take up residence and literally suck the life out of homes and their families in their ardent quest to make friends.

Bonzers – *Good, wonderful, great.*

Bonzo – *Amazing, unbelievable.*

Borderless Reef – A spherical sandbar of corals and seaweed with no discernible edge; located in the Nebulous Nebula.

Brute^ – Squallix on-field player primarily responsible for felling opponents; purely a defensive position. "Predisposed to violence, and notoriously bad sports, brutes [are] prohibited from attempting to score as the likelihood of failed-shot frustration leading to butchery [outweighs] the benefits of a brute successfully landing a shot." [source: Everett Sheffield]

Bugalugs – Term of endearment, usually as pertains to a child or someone inattentive.

Byzantine gold – For a brief time considered the most valuable tangible, tradable commodity in the Omniverse. Tea (usually in brick form) now eclipses all other forms of currency.

Cerebral gymnastics – A competitive form of mental exercise. The game of chess falls into this category.

Colossal Misunderstanding, the – An event during which all of the planets located in the Bullfrog Galaxy were detonated and exploded into smithereens. It came about when the galaxy's Minister of Tourism suggested a catchy and upbeat promotional campaign to increase the number of visitors to the area. He said something to the effect of "We need to do something to get this sector to blow up" … as in "grab attention." His meaning was misunderstood.

Consarn it!" – Dimension Q Wild West expletive; a common phrase among prospectors and fellows who never get the girl.

Conveyant – A multidirectional escalator; the primary mode of transport to the academy's strata.

Crux – A subterranean arena below The Hub that accesses all of the Ocademy's elemental estates. Officially used only for Druther's Day. Unofficially used for a variety of illicit activities.

Demythtify – Debunk; get to the truth of a matter after sweeping away myth and legend.

Domesticrat – Robotic orb, a member of the academy service staff.

Fair dinks – *Okay, sounds good, genuine, true*; it once meant *good job*.

Galilean Games – A sporting competition comprised of numerous individual athletic endeavors and squad matches, held every jai (5) seekkl (years) in Dim Zeta; exhibitions include Pachinko, competitive eating, shooting fish in a barrel, speed diaper changing.

Gnook Gnome – One of a troop of hard-working culinary wizards who make the Ocademy meals served in the Gnook (Comestibles Commons).

Hammock – Bed constructed of a mesh sling suspended by cords; a person reposing in a hammock rather looks like a hot dog in a bun.

Holovid – Moving holographs, akin to the relationship of still photographs to videos but on a holo level.

HRu Hule Huli (or Hule Huli) – Omniversal cheer to which Squaller's add the phrase "a Squaller's life for me."

Illumination strata – Also called Illumo, the general term refers to the 2 strata of the Ocademy grounds that house the classrooms and library.

Knock your comet's tail out of orbit" – A term indicating you will be amazed or surprised by something you are about to learn, see, hear, taste, smell, touch, or experience.

Kwarp – Pi (3.14) light years, a light year being the distance a beam of light travels in a year. In Dim Q terms it is 5.9 trillion miles. Thus, a kwarp is approximately 18.5+ trillion miles or about 30 trillion kilometers.

Load of barnacles" – Aquin term for *nonsense, malarkey, baloney, hooey*.

Magno Silentium, the Great Hush – 1213 R.C.; the entire sekkl dedicated to silent reflection in gratitude for the end of an aeon-long uncivil war in various pockets of the Omniverse.

Mana* – Respect, esteem, reverence.

Merfolk – Sea denizens with human heads and torsos, fish tail bottom halves.

Omnicast – Hologram news broadcast delivered in unnervingly close proximity to the current location of an academy denizen.

Outernship – A scholastic activity whereby a student studies a specific discipline onsite (off campus) for a term.

Pachinko – Urban tumbling, high-rise-scaling, and structure diving. Dim Q has recently appropriated the sport and renamed it Parkour.

Pan-Element Fusion – A social movement dedicated to harmony and interaction among the elements.

PBJ – A simple and simply delightful Dim Q food item whereby a piece of bread (baked wheat product) is smeared with peanuts pummeled into a paste, along with heartlessly eviscerated fruit; stands for Peanut Butter & Jelly.

Quag – Short for quagmire, muck, crowd, mess.

Rattle your dags" – *Hurry up, pick up the pace, chop chop!*

Redshift – A Doppler shift proportional to distance and recession velocity as related to the displacement of wavelengths at the red end of the spectrum; the appearance of cosmological entities moving away from observers; as opposed to blueshift.

Reinventing the Wheel ... Again – Widgetry textbook by Miss Eeng Leenk.

Rellies – Relatives, family members, blood relations; those who embarrass us ruthlessly and unrelentingly and show up unannounced at the most inopportune of times.

Sandwich – A substantial foodstuff comprised of a pair of slices of bread between which are *sandwiched* ingredients; most often including meat, cheese, vegetables, and condiments. While most sandwiches skew savory, the combination of peanut butter and jam is exceptionally popular. Owing to their portability, sandwiches are a favorite midday meal among working folk. When cut small with crusts removed (for tea service) these finger-sized treats miraculously lose all their calories.

Sea monkeys – Brine shrimp aquarium pets, a source of entertainment and amusement for families in all elements other than Aquis.

Shaper^ – Squallix coach.

Spavel – Ocademy class dealing with time-space travel and continuum continuity.

Sparga – Planet in the Surging Sea galactic cluster.

Sphinx – Regal age-old creature having the head of a human, the body of a lion, and large wings. The breed tends to be fond of jewelry and gourmet viands. They generally do not like to be touched.

Spiff – A small unit of time, too quick to measure.

Splendiferest – *Best, most wonderful, sublimest.*

Spunt – A harsh term meaning to curse, condemn, or damn.

Squad – Team, squadron, crew, platoon, cadre. This term is most often used at the Ocademy in reference to those participating in athletics.

Squaller^ – One who participates in the sport of Squallix, specifically a field player.

Squallix^ – A competitive Aquatic sport involving hippocampi, dwarf kraken, puffer fish, and hippocamp riders; the amateur leagues are known as Aspirant Squallix; the pro ranks are called the Vocs (short for vocational).

Squallix in Our Time^ – Seasonal publication highlighting Squallix players and techniques. Note, the majority of the magazine is devoted to merchandise advertising.

Strangulater – A swath of cloth tied around the neck of a sentient (with a neck) to remind him/her/its/hemm of his/her/its/hemm responsibilities and duties; also called a necktie.

Sub-frequency – Only Aethereans, dolphins, canines, and sub-sub-woofer speakers are able to pick up this low-frequency wave vibration.

Surging Sea galactic cluster – A highly mobile and active area of Dim Alpha containing a nursery for stars.

Swizzle-Burman Six-Color Wheel – The full spectrum of light and pigment harnessed into six definable sections; the omniversal symbol of interdimensional inclusion.

Teatricor – One who portrays other beings or fictional characters as a form of entertainment, paid or otherwise (most often *otherwise*); an actor; a derisive term for one who either lives with his/her/its/hemm parents as an adult and/or is deluded and destitute.

Tena koe" – A Maori (New Zealand aboriginal) greeting, used when addressing an individual.

Thank the Aethereans" – A phrase used to acknowledge good fortune; often a follow-up to "Aethereans take me away," uttered after things have worked out and calm down.

Tray jack – A portable folding contraption used by waiters upon which to sit heavy food trays. In cases where diners are badly behaved, whingy, or ungrateful, the trays may be flung at the diners and the jacks used for bashing.

Tuxedo – A formal set of clothing specific to planet Gaia, usually worn by males, most often by humans, although originated by penguins.

Twixt-term hiatus – The break between class terms at the Ocademy.

Ultra-Aetherean light – A wavelength on the luminance spectrum capable of piercing or illuminating the densest darkness and showing things generally obscured from sight. Since ante-antiquity, Nonn has been attempting to peculate this form of radiance from the Aethereans and has employed bandits, moles, and hitmen to this end. Thus far, his efforts have been unsuccessful.

Unexpected Inquisition, the – Instituted when a rigorous tollway system was installed along the ley lines, those seeking to advance beyond a given toll station were spontaneously subjected to a series of difficult and sometimes personal questions, such as those posed to King Arthur as relayed by lauded British historians Monty Python: "What is your name? What is your quest? What is the airspeed velocity of an unladen swallow?" Note, it's best to have a firm grasp of your favorite color prior to traveling the ley lines.

Unicorn – Magical horse with a horn extending from its forehead, believed to have healing powers.

Valet – A domestic attendant responsible for the dress, appearance, and overall outfitting of the sentient in its care.

Vilranyuh*" – *Thank you, merci, danke, gracias, grazie.*

Volumes and Verses – Ocademy book shop.

W.C. – The letters stand for water closet, a personal hygiene room containing a sink and flushable toilet, sometimes along with a bathtub or shower.

Wand – An extraordinary device capable of eliciting music, magic, musical magic, or magical music. Forget the gift card, give a wand!

Ward – A first- through fifth-level Fiddlehead.

Waterbed, waterchair, watersofa, et al – Furniture (generally designed to uphold bodies) that is filled with water as a means of fluid stability, rendering the item exceptionally comfortable.

Wheel, the – On the upper Illumination stratum, the central area that leads to the Ocademy fruit sectors where classes are conducted.

Whillions – The numerical measurement following bajillions.

Wiksto" – An enthusiastic exclamatory phrase indicating the planned occurrence of something wonderful or magical.

Wonder Bread – The carved bakery item referred to in the phrase "the greatest thing since sliced bread."

Now prepare to dive into the next installment of Pete's story

Here Be Kraken

Made in the USA
Columbia, SC
29 August 2023

22159639R10062